商務英文簡報
技巧全攻略

Making Presentations in English

作者・Ian Andrew McKinnon
翻譯・羅竹君／鄭家文
審訂・Judy Majewski

完美掌握簡報起承轉合
打造驚豔全場的英文簡報

- 循序漸進的簡報步驟
- 精錬實用的簡報金句
- 模擬商務實境的範例
- 精美繽紛的彩圖頁面

Plan A

Plan B

目錄 CONTENTS

PART 5 PHRASES FOR CONCLUDING YOUR PRESENTATION
總結簡報的語句

PREPARING FOR YOUR PRESENTATION

簡報前的準備工作

一場成功的簡報有賴於完善的準備。首先,你可以藉由以下六項必要的準備步驟,建構腦中的想法:

 UNIT 1 Learning About the Audience
認識簡報對象

 UNIT 2 Assembling the Outline
製作簡報綱要

 UNIT 3 Creating Your Own Outline
建立個人的簡報大綱

 UNIT 4 Preparing the Format
設計綱要型態

 UNIT 5 Enhancing Your Delivery
加強表達方式

 UNIT 6 Practicing the Presentation
簡報模擬練習

UNIT 1 Learning About the Audience
認識簡報對象

得到簡報主題後,你應該盡可能地對簡報對象具備各方面的認識。

1. Politics, culture, and language 了解聽眾的政治、文化、語言背景
2. Professional backgrounds 職業背景
3. Technical knowledge 專業知識
4. Opinions and values 想法與價值觀
5. Methods of background information research 研究背景知識的方法

1 Politics, culture, and language
了解聽眾的政治、文化、語言背景

做簡報的最終目標,是**清楚地傳遞主題訊息**,而要成功地達到此一目標,與聽講者建立良好的關係是其關鍵。如果能在事前對聽眾的政治、文化及語言背景做一番了解,便能和他們建立更加和諧的關係。

1 Are there any cultural or political topics that you want to highlight or stay away from?
是否有要特別提出或避免提及的主題?

2 Will engaging the audience with questions be offensive or inappropriate?
提問是否恰當?

3 Is humor appropriate or not? And if so, what kind?
是否該表現幽默?
要用哪種方式?

4 Are there other non-native speakers in the audience? Will you have to simplify your language?
是否有外籍聽眾?是否需簡化演講用語?

2 Professional backgrounds 職業背景

　　簡報對象詳細的職業背景是很珍貴的資訊，了解他們的工作角色、職位及職務內容，能幫助你設定報告的內容及表達方式。

1
Does the audience include salespeople, technicians, managers, or entry-level staff?
聽眾的職業及位階為何？

2
Have any audience members been employed by other major companies?
聽眾曾任職其他公司嗎？

3
Are there any mutual relationships with previous employers?
聽眾與前雇主間的互動關係為何？

3 Technical knowledge 專業知識

　　另一項與聽眾有關的資訊，是他們對簡報主題瞭解的深度。知道聽眾的專業知識，能讓你以適當程度的語言傳遞資訊——當簡報內容涉及專門知識時更是如此。

1
How familiar is your audience with the technical parts of your presentation?
聽眾對簡報主題的了解程度為何？

2
What is the audience's area of expertise/level of education?
聽眾的專業和教育程度為何？

3
How many years of experience in the field does the audience have?
聽眾在該產業領域的年資和經驗為何？

4 Opinions and values 想法與價值觀

 亞里斯多德曾說:「The fool persuades me with his reasons; the wise man persuades me with my own.(愚者以己理說服他人,智者以聽者之理說服其人。)」

以下是一些深入的問題,讓你仔細思考簡報對象具備的觀念價值:

① 聽眾對主題所持的立場

What is the audience's position regarding the subject matter?
➤ Is your audience already for or against what you are going to say?

② 聽眾對簡報者的感覺

How does the audience feel about you as the presenter?
➤ Are there people in the audience who know you?

③ 聽眾對簡報較偏向懷疑或支持?

Will audience members be skeptical or supportive?
➤ What are the audience's expectations?

④ 聽眾習慣的簡報方式

What kind of presentation is the audience used to?
➤ What is the audience's standard of excellence?

⑤ 聽眾出席是出於自願或被強迫?

Are audience members attending because they want to be here?
➤ Do they actually care about what you have to say?

⑥ 聽眾想從簡報獲取什麼資訊?

How will audience members benefit from the presentation?
➤ Can you give them valuable information?

⑦ 什麼資訊對聽眾最有益?

What kind of information will be valuable to this particular audience?
➤ What motivates the audience?
➤ How can audience members be inspired to act or buy?

5 Methods of background information research
研究背景知識的方法

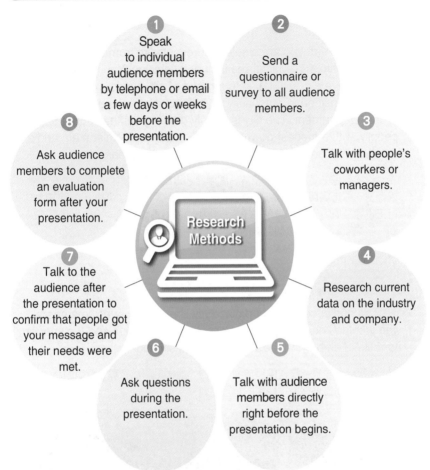

1. 在簡報進行的幾天或幾週前，透過電話或電子郵件，和參與的聽眾進行個別對話。
2. 寄問卷或調查表給所有的聽眾。
3. 和聽眾的同事或主管交談。
4. 對簡報對象的產業和公司進行研究。
5. 在簡報即將進行前的空檔，與聽眾直接對談。
6. 在簡報進行時提出問題。
7. 做完簡報後立刻與聽眾交談，確認你的訊息有確實傳遞，以及他們的需求有獲得滿足。
8. 做完簡報後，請聽眾做一份意見調查表。

Scenario 模擬情境

Imagine that you are a sales representative from an American car dealership that specializes in hybrid vehicles. You have been asked to give a presentation to a group of city council members who are considering purchasing hybrid vehicles for the city's Public Works Department. The city is rapidly growing and has about 82,000 people, with a modest downtown core, many parks, clean air, and a number of booming commercial and residential areas.

假設你是一名業務，服務於一間專賣油電車的美國汽車經銷商。公司要求你對一群市議員做簡報，他們正在考慮為工務局添購油電車。你所在的城市正迅速發展，人口約八萬二千人，市中心的位置大小適中，市內有許多公園，空氣新鮮，也有數個繁榮的商業及住宅區。

The Audience 簡報對象

The audience is a group of mostly liberal city council members who want to know the general benefits of hybrid cars and the specific benefits of employing the vehicles in this situation.

簡報的對象是一群作風開放的市議員，他們希望能了解油電車的基本優點，以及其在這種情境下使用的特別益處。

General Benefits 優勢說明

Cheaper operating costs 營運成本低廉

It costs almost $940 less per year to run a hybrid car (assuming 15,000 miles of driving per year).

營運一輛油電車，一年的花費不到 940 美元（假設每年哩程數為 15,000 英里）。

Audience-specific benefit 聽眾可享有的益處

The cheaper operating costs of hybrid cars will save money for the city's taxpayers.

油電車便宜的燃料費，能節省運用該市納稅人所繳的稅金。

Better mileage 更佳的性能表現

In ideal conditions, a hybrid car is capable of 45.83 miles per gallon.

在最佳狀態下，僅一加侖的油能讓油電車跑 45.83 公里的距離。

Less air pollution 減少空氣汙染

Hybrid cars can reduce air pollution by 90 percent.

油電車能減少 90% 的空氣汙染量。

Less global warming 降低全球暖化

Increased fuel efficiency also results in lower production of carbon dioxide, a major factor in global warming.

燃料使用效能增加可以減少全球暖化主因——二氧化碳的排放量。

Assembling the Outline
製作簡報綱要

一旦對簡報對象有了清楚的認識，你應該仔細思考，希望藉由這個簡報主題，在聽眾身上達到什麼效果，接著決定內容大綱。本章節為你介紹一般簡報類型中四種可應用的綱要。

1. Introducing a new product 介紹新產品
2. Recommending a new policy 推薦新政策
3. Reporting on research 研究報告
4. Reporting on feasibility 可行性報告

1 Introducing a new product 介紹新產品

本類型簡報的主要目的，是**說服消費者購買產品**，而達到目的之方法，為**說明產品的特色與優點。**

此簡報的內容，在於為消費者說明產品價值，或針對市場狀況為他們提供一些背景知識。但需特別注意的是，簡報的主要結構應該要清楚說明產品特性和優點。

① Introduction 簡介	**a** 自我介紹 **b** 引言、主旨及內容綱要
② Value Proposition 價值引導	該產品對顧客最有益的核心價值
③ Market Background 市場資訊	產品市場的現狀
④ Product Positioning 產品定位	產品最特別的賣點
⑤ Features and Benefits 產品特色及優點	**a** 性能規格　　　　　　**e** 和其他產品的相容性 **b** 吸引顧客的產品特色　**f** 未來升級擴充的可能性 **c** 與特定客群間的關連性　**g** 產品的風格 **d** 該產品如何增進顧客的生活機能
⑥ Conclusion 結論	重申簡報主旨

2 Recommending a new policy 推薦新政策

此類簡報的主要目的在於**告知聽眾**，他們**從事某件事的原因**。

謹記，此類型的簡報結構，是**從聽眾已知的內容**（相關背景知識問題），流暢地**引導至他們所不知道的部分**（你提出的解決之道）。

① Introduction 簡介
- a 自我介紹
- b 引言、主旨及內容綱要

② Background 背景知識
- a 說明現狀或面臨的問題
- b 提出問題來源
- c 提出問題的嚴重性
- d 解釋問題背後的論據
- e 定義基本專業術語

③ Problem 提出問題
- a 定義你要解決的問題
- b 敘述要義或重點（重述簡介的內容）

④ Solution 解決方案
- a 解釋你會如何解決問題
- b 根據你提出的解決方法，預測正反兩面的結果
- c 說明採用推薦方案的可能成效

⑤ Methods 程序
- a 說明欲達成目標的詳細步驟
- b 明言你會採取何種方法達成目標

⑥ Time Schedule 時間表
- 指出你計畫要何時完成每一項方案

⑦ Conclusion 結論
- a 根據先前下的結論，說明成果代表的意義
- b 重申你的主旨

⑧ Recommendations 推薦
- 根據結論，聽眾應該採取哪些行動？

3 Reporting on research 研究報告

在商業、科學技術的領域中，此類型是最常見的簡報類型，其目的是**教育**，至於簡報方為**從研究結果提出結論**。

根據原創或引用的實驗結果，提出高科技研究的成果報告，往往是進行此類簡報最傳統的架構：

1 Introduction
簡介

- **a** 自我介紹
- **b** 引言、主旨及內容綱要

2 Background
背景知識

文獻回顧

3 Methods and Materials
研究方法和材料

- **a** 實驗設計（若在介紹背景知識時沒有解釋到，在此提出研究方法根據的理論）
- **b** 使用材料
- **c** 實驗步驟

4 Results
結果

- **a** 第一次實驗結果
- **b** 第二次實驗結果
- **c** 第三次實驗結果

5 Discussion of Results
討論實驗結果

- **a** 針對每一次實驗結果的特異之處提出說明
- **b** 對聽眾強調每一項實驗之特殊重要性

6 Conclusion
結論

- **a** 根據前面的說明下結論，討論這些結果代表什麼意義？
- **b** 重申你的主旨

7 Recommendations
推薦

根據結論，聽眾應該採取哪些行動？

4 Reporting on feasibility 可行性報告

　　不管工作行業為何，都需要進行評估報告，它也往往是商業計畫的一部分。這一類型簡報的主要目的是**判定提議的投資計畫是否有成功的潛力**，進行方式則是**調查評定**規畫這項投資的**各種方法**，推薦最適合的一個。

1 Introduction 簡介	**a** 自我介紹 **b** 引言、主旨及內容綱要
2 Reasons for conducting the study 進行研究的原因	**a** 是為了誰而研究？ **b** 為何他們需要這項研究？ **c** 他們的需求為何？
3 Background 背景知識	**a** 提供其歷史背景 **b** 解釋現有的系統 **c** 新提議的系統內容 **d** 相關理論
4 Problem 提出問題	**a** 檢視標準 　• 哪些基準是解決問題需要做到的？ 　• 需要達到哪些標準才能做到可行的解決方案？ 　　（成本、設計的考量等） **b** 問題的範圍 **c** 研究涵蓋的主題 **d** 研究的限制 **e** 基本假定
5 Discussion 討論	**a** 方案**A** 　（• 說明方案內容　• 評價與分析） **b** 方案**B** 　（• 說明方案內容　• 評價與分析）
6 Conclusion 結論	**a** 根據評價與分析的結果，哪一項是最佳方案？ **b** 是否會產生任何缺失？ **c** 該項方案是否可行（根據成本和其他標準分析）？ **d** 重申簡報主旨
7 Recommendations 推薦	根據先前的結論，聽眾該如何選擇？

Creating Your Own Outline
建立個人的簡報大綱

儘管大多數簡報不出〈Unit 2〉提到的四大類型（介紹新產品、推薦新政策、研究報告、可行性報告），還是有些簡報需要更特殊的綱要設計。本章節將說明建立個人簡報大綱的三項技巧。

1. Defining type, objective, and method 界定簡報類型、簡報目的及簡報方法
2. Brainstorming with mind maps 用「心智圖」激盪腦力
3. Turning your mind map into an outline 將心智圖轉化為簡報大綱
4. Choosing suitable software for making your slides 選擇適合的軟體製作你的投影片

Defining type, objective, and method
界定簡報類型、簡報目的及簡報方法

要設定自己的簡報大綱，第一步就是先**評估報告主題**，決定簡報的**類型**、**目標**跟**方法**。

想找出這些關鍵內容，你可以問問自己三個問題：

What type of presentation is this?
簡報類型為何？

What is your objective with this audience?
你希望在簡報對象身上達到什麼目標？

What is the best method for accomplishing this objective?
達到這個目標的最佳方法為何？

回答這三個問題後，你的簡報主題會變得更完整，你也會更容易設定簡報大綱。

EXAMPLE Ⓐ

Scenario 模擬情境

You represent a consulting firm that has done original research on both the production and the market feasibility of a product that your audience wants to produce and sell.

你代表一間顧問公司，為簡報對象希望生產販售的商品進行生產及市場可行性的初步研究。

❶ **What type of presentation is this?** 簡報類型為何？	這種簡報型態，混和了〈Unit 2〉所提四種報告型態（介紹新產品、推薦新策略、研究報告、可行性評估）中的兩種： ⓐ 研究報告 ⓑ 可行性評估
❷ **What is your objective with this audience?** 你希望在簡報對象身上達到什麼目標？	ⓐ 提供商品生產過程的訊息 ⓑ 對投資方案的可行性提出建議 ➤ 提供聽眾商品生產及其可行性的相關訊息
❸ **What is the best method for accomplishing this objective?** 達到這個目標的最佳方法為何？	ⓐ 對生產程序進行研究 ⓑ 研究讓該投資方案可行的各種方法 ➤ 根據生產過程和可行性研究的結果提出結論

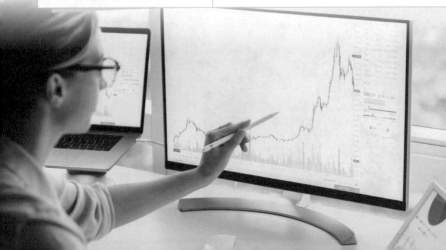

Scenario 模擬情境

Imagine that you are a real estate agent selling a block of five brand-new condominiums in a prime location. Each condo has four stories, with roof access and skylights on the top floor, six bedrooms, four bathrooms, a kitchen/dining room, a two-car garage, and a small front yard with grass and a security gate.

A new high-speed rail station is close by, as well as a national freeway interchange. Shopping centers, schools, parks, and temples in the vicinity are among the best in the city. A huge science park that employs several thousand people is only 30 minutes away. On clear days when the wind is strong, the not-so-distant mountains provide a scenic vista when viewed from the roof.

設想你是一位房地產經紀人,在高級地段銷售共計五棟的全新的公寓大廈。每一棟大廈有四層樓,並設有通往頂樓的通道,頂樓有天窗可以眺望星光;一共有六間臥房、四間衛浴、一間廚房和餐廳、一座可容納兩部車的車庫、小草坪前院,以及警衛駐守的大門。

全新的高鐵車站和高速公路交流道就在附近,鄰近地區的購物中心、學校、公園和廟宇都是市區裡最頂尖的,而擁有十幾萬工作人口的科學園區,距離公寓只有30分鐘的路程。遇到天晴風輕時,站在屋頂上便能享受不遠處群山的美好景色。

The Audience 簡報對象

The audience has assembled at your hastily constructed office in a dusty lot next to the condos. The group contains potential buyers who have responded to fliers you handed out to people in cars stopped at busy intersections during the last month. Some people have arrived in luxury cars, but most are driving midrange automobiles or scooters. One car arrives carrying a family of five and a large, but well-behaved, dog. Almost all the audience members are couples, and more than a few have brought their children.

The point of the flier that audience members have responded to is that these condos will increase in value tremendously in a short time because of their great location and the rapid development in the area.

簡報的對象聚集在公司匆忙興建的辦公室，它位於公寓旁灰塵密布的工地中。這群人包含建案的潛在顧客，他們在上個月開車等十字路口時收到了你的傳單，並因此有了回應。雖然有些人是開著豪華轎車抵達，但大部分與會者都是開普通汽車或是騎機車。其中一台車載著一家五口和一隻溫馴乖巧的大狗前來。聽眾幾乎都是夫婦，有許多夫婦甚至帶著孩子一起參加。

讓他們產生興趣的的傳單內容著重於公寓的短期增值潛力，這是由於公寓地點絕佳，加上鄰近區域的快速發展所致。

❶ Presentation Type 簡報類型

Introduction to a new product
介紹新產品

❷ The Objective 在簡報對象身上達到的目標

To convince potential buyers to purchase a condo
說服買家（簡報對象）購買房屋

❸ Best Method 最佳方式

Explain the features and benefits of the condos
解說房屋的特色及優點

Scenario 模擬情境

Imagine that you are the owner/operator of a famous dumpling restaurant. Over the years, your restaurant has been featured many times in the "Top 10" list of local newspapers. Dumplings have recently become trendy overseas, and a foreign businessman has asked you to become his partner in a chain of restaurants in America.

The time has come to train a group of would-be managers in the fine art of making your delicious dumplings. Your ingredients and methods have been a closely guarded secret for years, but the time has come to share your dumpling knowledge and capitalize on this business opportunity.

假設你是一間知名餃子館的老闆，過去幾年來你的餐廳一直在當地報紙上的美食評鑑名列前十大。最近餃子在國外突然變得非常風行，一名美國連鎖餐廳的外籍企業家邀請你與他合作。

現在是把你製作美味水餃的技術傳授出去、訓練儲備管理人員的時候了。多年來你對食物配方和烹調方法一直非常保密，不過現在應該把你對水餃的知識分享出來，為事業發展進行投資。

The Audience 簡報對象

The audience is a group of experienced chefs who will become managers. The chefs come from all across America and are eager to learn your ways. They are expecting detailed instructions so they can eventually train the employees in their restaurants. The chefs in the audience are all quite proud of their cooking skills, but they aren't familiar with making dumplings.

Your main objective is to describe the different varieties and ingredients of dumplings, as well as the production processes and expected flavors, textures, and aromas so the audience can reproduce them. Your audience is gathered in the kitchen, where you have all your ingredients, utensils, and equipment for dumpling production.

簡報的對象是一群經驗豐富的廚師，之後他們會開始管理餐廳。這些廚師來自全美各地，非常渴望學習你的手藝。他們希望能夠聽到詳細的說明，之後才能訓練自己餐廳裡的員工。這些廚師對於自己的烹飪技術都非常有自信，不過對於水餃的製作卻不甚熟悉。

這次簡報最主要的目的是向他們介紹各種口味的水餃、不同的材料和製作方式，以及特定的味道、口感和香氣，如此一來他們才能做出最道地的水餃。現在你的聽眾全都在聚集在廚房裡，一切做水餃的食材用具都準備就緒了。

❶ Presentation Type 簡報類型

Instruction and demonstration of a process
指導和示範製作餃子的過程

❷ The Objective 欲達成的目標

To educate the chefs so they can make dumplings correctly
教導廚師，讓他們學會正確製作餃子的方法

❸ Best Method 最佳方式

Teaching the chefs by example
實際示範做餃子給廚師看

2 Brainstorming with mind maps 用「心智圖」激盪腦力

「心智圖」(mind map)是一種腦力激盪，能幫助你**設立簡報大綱**，並整理各種絕佳的創意。因此，簡報的**類型、目標、方法**都可以利用心智圖規畫設計。可利用**線條、色彩、符號、樹狀圖**等顯示關連性，為您的心智圖加入個人風格。

心智圖的主要優點在於能鼓勵創意，不做直線思考，讓思想的發展不受固定的因果或模式限制，能夠更自在地激發新的想法。如果你有較多時間，可以先跳脫心智圖進行推想，過一會兒再回來繼續。

Step 1 在一張紙上寫下**簡報的目標**，並把目標畫個框圈起來。

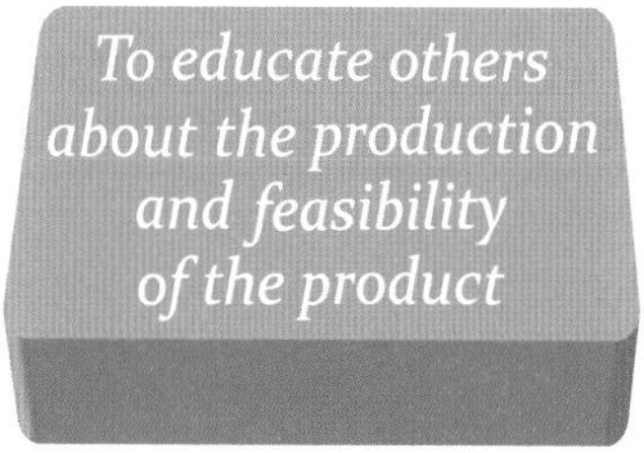

> To educate others
> about the production
> and feasibility
> of the product

Step 2 在框起來的目標旁邊，寫下**完成目標的方法**，將每一種方法圈起來，並畫線將這些方法與目標連在一起。

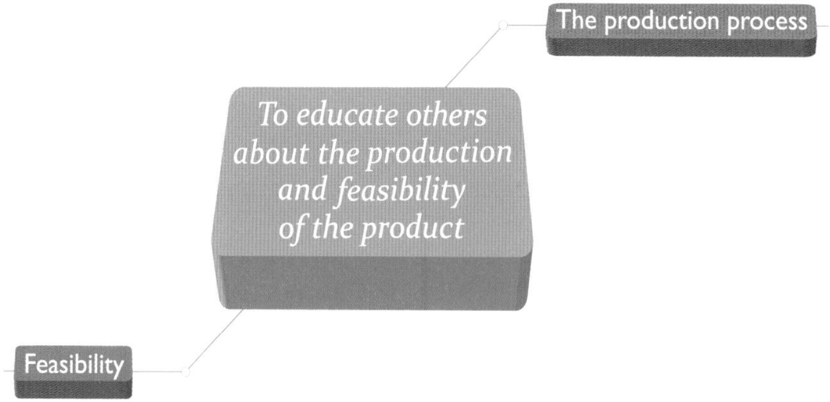

> The production process
>
> To educate others
> about the production
> and feasibility
> of the product
>
> Feasibility

Step 3 針對這些方法做更多**細節說明**，內容越詳細越好。

Step ④ 寫下你腦中的每種意見，修正內容後再選出最佳的意見。
這一步驟的重點是盡量**激盪出最多相關的想法**。

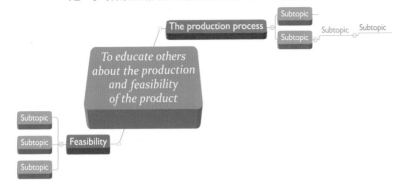

Step ⑤ 在每一項新的想法間**尋找關連性**，並畫線顯示彼此的連結關
係。當心智圖開始越變越大，就利用數字或符號組織這些想
法，讓它們彼此間具有邏輯順序。

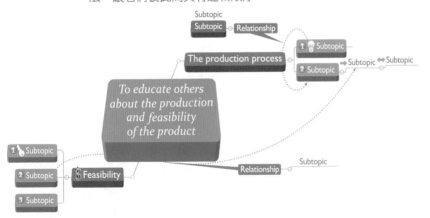

Step ⑥ 當你開始覺得所有好主意都已經用盡，或是認為所有與簡報主
旨相關的內容都已經包含在內，就可以回到目標主題，根據所
有新增的訊息**重新進行分析**。

Step ⑦ 根據分析結果**調整心智圖**，如有必要，修改目標主題，重新尋
找與相關意見之間的關連，同時要確認所有論據內容都與主題
相關，且數據或邏輯都很精確。

> ★ 好用的心智圖軟體：Xmind: www.xmind.net
> Coggle: coggle.it.

3 Turning your mind map into an outline
將心智圖轉化為簡報大綱

要製作個人的簡報綱要，只需要垂直地組織你的心智圖即可。

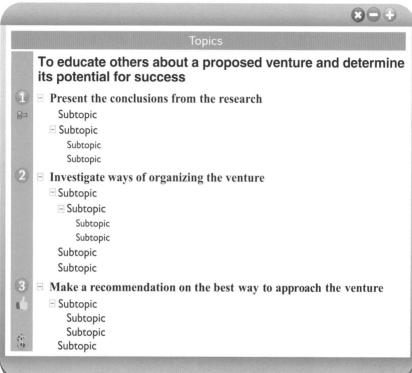

Topics

To educate others about a proposed venture and determine its potential for success

1. ☐ **Present the conclusions from the research**
   - Subtopic
   - ☐ Subtopic
     - Subtopic
     - Subtopic

2. ☐ **Investigate ways of organizing the venture**
   - ☐ Subtopic
     - ☐ Subtopic
       - Subtopic
       - Subtopic
     - Subtopic
     - Subtopic

3. ☐ **Make a recommendation on the best way to approach the venture**
   - ☐ Subtopic
     - Subtopic
     - Subtopic
   - Subtopic

Presentation Equipment 簡報器材

1 projector 投影機
2 projection screen 投影螢幕
3 whiteboard 白板
（interactive whiteboard 互動式白板）
4 laser pointer 雷射筆
5 flip chart 簡報架
6 wireless microphone 無線麥克風

7 markers 白板筆
8 eraser 板擦
9 cable 傳輸線
10 laptop 筆電
11 tablet 平板電腦
12 plug 插頭

4 Choosing suitable software for making your slides
選擇適合的軟體製作你的投影片

以下是幾種常見的投影片製作軟體：

PowerPoint

- 功能完善
- 最常見的簡報軟體

Prezi

- 轉頁、縮放的效果像動畫
- 適用於介紹流程、組織

(來源：*https://prezi.com/*)

Canva

- 簡單易學
- 樣本、版面、圖庫的選擇多樣

(來源：*https://www.canva.com/en/*)

Emaze

- 可製作 3D 簡報
- 模板精美

（來源：*https://www.emaze.com/*）

Powtoon

- 便於製作動畫
- 提供免版權音樂

（來源：*https://www.powtoon.com/*）

Adobe Spark

- 簡單易學
- 內建漂亮圖庫

4 Preparing the Format
設計綱要型態

簡報時不能把綱要裡所有的資訊都放到投影片上，在聽眾面前一句句唸出來了事，
這種簡報將無法引起他們的注意。

將簡報大綱轉換成投影片是最重要的步驟，你必須將**綱要轉化成有趣的設計**，讓聽眾跟
得上報告的速度，抓住他們的注意力，但必須謹記，**良好的口語表達能力**才是成功簡報
的關鍵。你的投影片裡只需要放**簡報的關鍵重點和輔助圖片**。

1. Guidelines for laying out slides 投影片設計原則
2. Condensing your speech on your slides 將演說內容精簡地呈現在投影片上
3. Writing bullet points 撰寫條列式要點
4. Guidelines for presenting your slides 用投影片做簡報的原則
5. Charts and graphs for different purposes 利用圖表呈現不同類型的資料
6. Diagrams for different purposes 展現想法的各種圖表

1 Guidelines for laying out slides 投影片設計原則

製作投影片時，請記得六大原則。只要花點心思加些設計，你的簡報就能讓
人留下更深刻的印象。

1 Well-designed layout 良好的設計版面	• 主要訊息必須清楚明顯	
2 Simplicity 簡約	• 中性色調 • 不要在同一張投影片上放上太多資訊 • 使用相同的主題顏色，避免太鮮豔的顏色，以及多餘或複雜的圖像 • 有些版式太花俏，容易擾亂視聽，要避免與簡報主題不符的版式	
3 Consistency 一致性	• 用色與背景插圖互相搭配	
4 The 6-6-6 Rule 三個6原則	• 每個要點說明盡量不超過 **6 個字** • 每張投影片不超過 **6 個要點** • 每張投影片句子不超過 **6 行**	

⑤ The 7-second rule
7秒原則

- 每張投影片所傳達的訊息，必須讓聽眾在 **7 秒內**清楚了解

◀24字級

⑥ Font size and font type
字體大小與字型

- 不要使用小於 **24 字級**的字體
- 不要在投影片上用超過**三種以上**的字型
- 避免在單一投影片上使用太突兀的字
- 避免使用**粗體**、**斜體**，和**全部大寫**的英文字
- 字型簡單乾淨
- 每張投影片的標題字使用 **35-45** 的字級呈現

字體

▲35字級　▲45字級

EXAMPLE 從以下投影片指出版面設計的五個問題

使用大寫字型

圖片太花俏且與主題不符

THIS MONTH'S REAL ESTATE SALES CONTEST

- First prize: a Cadillac Eldorado
- Second prize: a set of steak knives
- Third prize: You're fired!

A-B-C. A-Always, B-Be, C-Closing.
Always be closing, Always be closing.
You want to know what it takes to
sell real estate?

Go home and play with your kids!　Isn't it great?

You get leads. Mitch & Murray paid good money. Get their numbers to call them.

字體太小

同張投影片上使用太多顏色

使用過多不同字型

2 Condensing your speech on your slides
將演說內容精簡地呈現在投影片上

　　所謂製作成功的簡報投影片，應該**涵蓋**你報告的**各項重點**，以最**易讀**的文字呈現。

　　假設你要報告以下這段話：

Our two main goals this year are to increase revenue by 70 percent to 80 percent and to maintain a small profit. Our strategies for achieving these goals are to grow our tablet market share and to crack the formidable U.S. market.

　　可以將其歸結成重點，以此投影片呈現：

Goals and strategies for 2021

- Increase revenue by 70 percent to 80 percent
- Maintain a small profit
- Grow tablet market share
- Crack the U.S. market

　　很多失敗的簡報就是在一張投影片裡塞入太多資訊，但其實製作簡報的基本概念就是越簡單越好。

★ 以下是把複雜頁面簡化的步驟：

Step 1

判斷版面是否太擠，一次放太多訊息且字太小，讓聽眾無法了解簡報重點。若太擠，可試著將內容分成二頁。

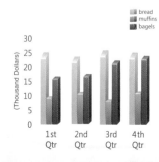

Doh! Bakery sales over the last 4 quarters

bread / muffins / bagels

(Thousand Dollars)
30
25
20
15
10
5
0

1st Qtr　2nd Qtr　3rd Qtr　4th Qtr

The most noticeable trend over the last four quarters is the steady increase in bagel sales. The main reason for the increased popularity among consumers is the introduction of a wider variety of flavors. The introduction of orange cranberry in the second quarter made the first noticeable difference. We believe that taste samples in the store have also made a difference, as has the bundling of discounted cream cheese.

將一頁的投影片內容分成二頁，圖表放在第一張投影片，圖表說明放到第二張投影片。簡化頁面，能在做口頭報告時，讓聽眾把注意力放在你身上。

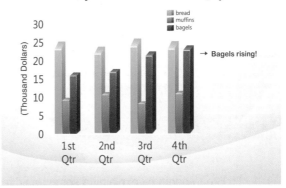

Doh! Bakery sales over the last 4 quarters

The most noticeable trend over the last four quarters is the steady increase in bagel sales. The main reason for the increased popularity among consumers is the introduction of a wider variety of flavors. The introduction of orange cranberry in the second quarter made the first noticeable difference. We believe that taste samples in the store have also made a difference, as has the bundling of discounted cream cheese.

Step 3

盡量將文字說明的部分，**條列**在投影片上以呈現重點。

Why have bagel sales gone up?

- The introduction of a wider variety of flavors

- The introduction of orange cranberry

- Taste samples in the store

- Bundling of discounted cream cheese

3 Writing bullet points 撰寫條列式要點

要注意的是，條列式要點通常是用**子句**表現，並不是完整的句子，因此**不加句號**。不過這類要點也能寫成完整的句子，甚至用問句表現；如果是完整句子，分項要點就必須加上標點符號。但無論你選擇用哪一種方式列出要點，前後文格式都必須一致，分項要點也要盡量精簡。

EXAMPLE

講稿 ▼

①   I'd like to begin by explaining some basic features of plug-in hybrid cars. They generate electricity with an onboard gasoline or diesel engine. But the battery can also be charged by plugging the car into an electric socket. The electric motor is designed to be the sole power source for low speeds and short distances, whereas the gasoline motor takes over at higher speeds on the freeway.

投影片 ▼

Basic features of plug-in hybrid cars

- Generate their own electricity via the gas engine
- Can be plugged into an electric socket
- Electric motor for slower speeds
- Gas motor takes over at higher speeds

EXAMPLE

講稿 ▼

②   Our goal for the long term is to increase our efforts toward developing plug-in hybrid vehicles. Plug-in hybrid cars are a top-priority program for our company because of the huge potential they offer for improved fuel economy. These cars provide significant opportunities to reduce pollution and reliance on petroleum.

投影片 ▼

Reasons for long-term development of plug-in hybrid cars

- Huge potential for improved fuel economy
- Reduced pollution
- Reduced reliance on petroleum

EXAMPLE ©

講稿 ▼

③　Other alternative fuel vehicles in the R&D stage include a car that runs on a mixture of 85% ethanol and 15% gasoline as well as fuel-cell vehicles, which use hydrogen to create electricity and emit only heat and water.

投影片 ▼

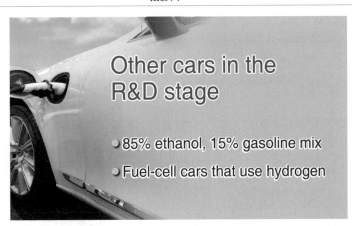

Other cars in the R&D stage

- 85% ethanol, 15% gasoline mix
- Fuel-cell cars that use hydrogen

4 Guidelines for presenting your slides
用投影片做簡報的原則

❶ 做簡報**不是悶著頭照著稿子唸**，預先做好練習，才能根據分項要點陳述內容。這種演說技巧會讓你的簡報能力突飛猛進。

❷ 投影片不僅是做給聽眾觀看的資料，也是你說明的提示。

❸ **不要背對聽眾**。調整電腦螢幕的位置，讓你可以面向電腦螢幕，而非面對投影布幕做簡報。

❹ 使用**無線滑鼠**可以讓你在簡報時四處走動。

❺ 如有需要可以使用**雷射筆**來指示投影片的內容。

❻ 如果你覺得某些資訊對聽眾來說太複雜又難記，可以將**文字資料**發給他們。

You have been asked to analyze the business practices of the small publishing company where you are employed as a secretary. The company finds both the authors and the buyers of the books it produces.

你在一間小型出版公司擔任秘書，公司要求你針對該企業實務進行分析，並找來公司合作的作者和書商聽你做簡報。

How can we improve business?

- Enhanced project planning and delivery
- Process improvement
- Effective sales and marketing

Oral Version

02

Our small business has lots of room for improvement. After analyzing the current situation, I found three main areas that we can work on. **First**, we need to enhance our project planning and delivery; too many book proposals lack sufficient quality and usefulness, and the end result is that they simply aren't marketable. **Second**, we have to improve the process, which means better communication and commitment of more resources to reviewing and editing. **Lastly**, our sales and marketing team needs to find more creative ways to reach customers, because we haven't found new clients in a long time. Now I'll go into more detail on each of these points.

You are presenting a technique for improving academic performance that will be taught at a six-hour workshop. To encourage students to sign up for the workshop, you are offering them a money-back guarantee of measurable results.

你在簡報中報告一種能增進學習效率的技巧課程,該課程將在長達六小時的研討會中教授,為了鼓勵學生參與該課程,你提出了沒效果就能退費的保證。

Oral Version

②   This brand-new memorization technique will improve your success in school. In just six hours, you'll gain an advantage over other students in three key ways.

First, expect a huge improvement in your academic planning and performance; **second**, we promise you'll be able to recall details faster, without having to double-check facts so often. That means speedier completion of assignments and quicker responses during class discussions. **Third**, your papers and research will be higher quality, and you'll be able to produce them in less time!

    Our confidence in the quality of this program is so strong that we offer a money-back guarantee of measurable results.

EXAMPLE ©

You are presenting an easy-to-use organizational software for project planning to a government agency. You offer free printers to the first 10 departments that purchase the software.

你要向政府機關介紹一款操作簡便的企畫軟體,同時提供免費的印表機給前十名購買的部門。

Enhance your government agency's productivity

- Complete projects and deliver services more quickly
- Enable interagency project planning
- Consolidate and simplify access to information

Oral Version

③ Government agency managers and just about everyone else will benefit from this easy-to-use organizational software. **To start**, you'll be completing projects more quickly and delivering services with more speed than ever before. **Also**, the potential for interagency project planning will be enabled by the easy sharing of complicated ideas. **Last but not least**, your agency will be able to consolidate and simplify access to information, easing everybody's workload.

5 Charts and graphs for different purposes
利用圖表呈現不同類型的資料

圖表最大的優勢，在於將要說明的數據以視覺效果呈現，而某些圖表特別適合表現特定種類的資訊。

1 Pie Chart　圓餅圖

圓餅圖最能表現**部分和整體的相對關係**，通常是用**百分比**的方式呈現。

SURVEY : FAVORITE ICE CREAM FLAVOR

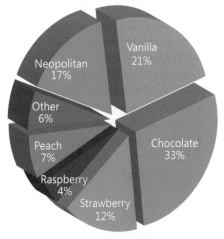

圖形分析

① Chocolate presents the **largest piece** of the pie.
巧克力佔了整張圓餅圖**最大的比例**。

② Raspberry is the favorite flavor of **a tiny portion** (4%) of the respondents.
覆盆子的比例為 4%，在最喜愛的口味當中只佔了**一小部分**。

③ Represented by the light yellow **wedge**, vanilla is the second most-popular ice cream flavor.
香草在這裡是淺黃的**扇形**，是第二受歡迎的口味。

★ 其他適合的主題：
market share（市場佔有率）、school grades（學校成績）

39

② Line Graph & Bar Graph 曲線圖和長條圖

曲線圖和長條圖可以表現**數字增長的趨勢**。

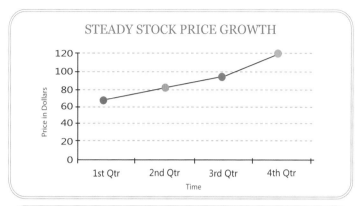

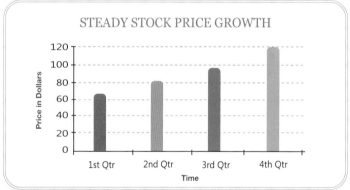

① You can see the line **rises steadily** throughout the year.
你可以看出曲線在一整年間**穩定上升**。

② The **final bar**, representing the fourth quarter, reaches $120.
代表第四季的**最後一道長條**，攀升至 120 元。

★ 其他適合的主題：
production efficiency（產能）、weekly exercise results（每週的運動成果）、financial growth（金融成長）

6 Diagrams for different purposes
展現想法的各種圖表

圖表不僅能表現統計數據，也能展現各個面向的生動概念和組織關係。

① Organization Diagram　組織圖

組織圖能夠表現**上下位階關係**，例如一間企業的員工結構。

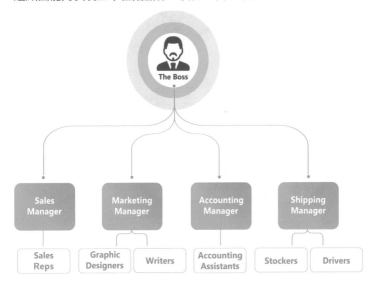

圖形分析

① The second level of the **hierarchy** represents middle management.
組織架構的第二層代表中階管理階層。

② **Both legs** under the Marketing Manager experience frequent personnel turnover.
行銷經理下層的**兩個分支**，人事汰換率很高。

③ At **the head of** the hierarchy, you'll find the boss.
在組織架構的**最上層**，是這家公司的老闆。

★ 其他適合的主題：
delegating responsibilities from a core authority（當權核心者分配職責）、
family tree（族譜）

② Cycle Diagram　循環圖

循環圖能夠表現**事物循環的過程**，例如商品輸送的循環流程。

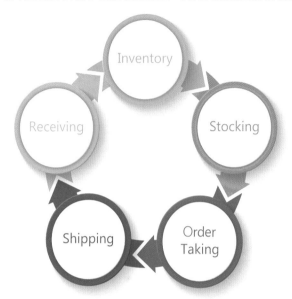

① The process **is cyclical**, as this diagram illustrates.
就如同圖表所展現，整個過程是**不斷循環的**。

② Five **segments** comprise the **model**.
此**模組**是由五個**部分**所組成。

③ Maintaining this **recurring model** is the key to our success.
維持此**模型的循環**是成功的關鍵。

④ Each **phase** is an indispensable part of the cycle.
每一個**階段**在流程中都是不可或缺的。

⑤ As long as the **cycle keeps repeating itself**, everything will be fine.
只要**整個過程不斷循環**，一切都不會有問題。

★ 其他適合的主題：
the four seasons（四季）、natural life cycle（大自然生命循環）

③ Radial Diagram　放射圖

放射圖能夠表現從**中心基準向外延伸**的關係，例如之前提過的**心智圖**或商品運輸路線。

圖形分析 ① All requests from the **branches** should be directed to **the hub**.
分部提出的所有要求，都應該直接傳達至**集散中心**。

② The Taipei main warehouse is the **core** of the operation.
台北倉庫是所有貨物運輸的**中心點**。

③ We can **radiate** instructions out to the branches from **HQ**.
我們可以從**總部**向各**分部**發布指示。

★ 其他適合的主題：
subway routes（地鐵路線）

Enhancing Your Delivery
加強表達方式

大多數人做簡報時都很難表現得自然，要站上台將整理好的訊息傳達給聽眾，會覺得緊張絕對是很自然的反應。

不過，還是有人能夠流暢自然地演說，全然吸引聽眾的注意力，這些溝通大師不僅能有效地將訊息傳達出去，同時還會讓我們覺得內容有趣、深具啟發性。其實流暢演說的關鍵就是自信，而具備自信的秘訣，就是完善的準備。

1. Good preparation 完善的準備
2. Delivery essentials 口語表達的重點
3. Language style 語言風格

1 Good preparation 完善的準備

在準備簡報的過程中，你會對簡報內容越來越熟悉，而**熟悉度越高，你就越不會感到緊張**。完善的準備包括投入足夠的時間和精力分析簡報對象、定義簡報目的和架構、設定大綱、製作 PowerPoint 檔案，最後還要準備一些適合簡報的實用語言。

究竟要花多久時間和精神準備才算恰當呢？其實只要讓「你」能克服緊張，就算是恰當。根據美國幽默大師馬克·吐溫的說法：「一場好的即席演講，要花上三個星期做準備。」

當然，每個人實際準備的時間會有很大的差距，但如果你從最基本的步驟開始做準備，你會對主題有深入的瞭解，也比較不容易感覺緊張。

以下是三個能夠減輕你心理負擔的訣竅：

1
提早抵達現場，和入場聽眾打招呼，這能讓你在簡報開始前，打破和聽眾間的冷漠關係。

2
在做簡報前找個時機做幾次深呼吸，從鼻子吸氣、嘴巴吐氣，開始前至少做六次。

3
如果你很緊張，不要說出來，聽眾或許根本不會注意到。

2 Delivery essentials 口語表達的重點

　　自信絕對是做簡報最重要的一環，但如果能同時做到以下六項要點，
聽眾對你的簡報會有更良好的反應：

① Appearance　外表

❶ 在簡報進行這類場合需要穿著**正式服裝**。
❷ 不要穿過於鮮豔花俏的服裝，會分散聽眾的注意力。
❸ 要特別注意個人的**儀容整潔**。

① 臉上的表情能夠傳達許多訊息，包括開心、熱忱、痛苦和傷感。
② 在做簡報時熱切又不失輕鬆的表情能達到最好的效果。
③ 一個能讓自己更注意臉部表情的方法，就是在講電話時看著鏡子，
　 或是在辦公桌上放個鏡子做練習。
④ **避免做出以下表情：**

 frown
鐵眉

表示你心情不佳。聽眾會記得你皺眉的神情，反而不易收到你要傳達的資訊。

 arched eyebrows
眉毛彎曲

會表達出驚訝、懷疑或疑惑的情緒。

 grimacing
扭曲的臉

表示你感受到痛苦的情緒。

 deadpan expression
撲克臉

讓你看起來無趣或讓人覺得你缺乏智慧。

 squint-eyed
瞇著眼睛

會讓人感覺不誠實或不值得信任。

③ Voice 聲調

❶ **提高音調**，讓後排的人也能聽到你的聲音，別對著前排的人輕聲細語。
❷ 注意不要發出太多「umm」和「ahh」之類的語助詞。
❸ 不可過度使用某些字詞如「like」和「you know」等。

④ Gestures 手勢

❶ 手勢很重要，有**加強語氣**的效果。
❷ 注重手臂、雙手，甚至頭部的動作。
❸ 利用雙手和手臂的姿勢表示**形狀和地點**。
❹ 朝外和朝上的手部動作，有**正面積極**的意味。

❺ 手掌打開、偶爾以手掌觸碰胸膛，會傳遞強烈**誠實**的訊息。

❻ 過多的手勢動作，即使是正向的意涵，也容易造成聽眾分心。

⑤ Body language 肢體語言

① 與聽眾面對面，**抬頭挺胸**站直。
② 沒有做手勢時雙臂放鬆，自然垂於身體兩側。

③ 避免做的動作包括：

A	B	C
把雙手放在臀部 hands on hips	雙手在背後交握 hands joined behind the back	雙手插口袋 hands in the pockets

D	E
雙臂交疊 crossed arms	坐著靠在椅背上 leaning back in a chair

⑥ Eye contact　眼神注視

① **直視聽眾雙眼**，建立信任和諧的關係。

② 環視室內各個角落，找到親切友善的臉龐後，先將**視線鎖定在他們身上**。

③ 一開始避免望向氣勢嚇人或冷漠的聽眾，等到簡報進入更深一層之後再朝向他們。

④ 盡可能和每一位聽眾做**眼神接觸**，讓他們贊同你的想法；**一次望向一位聽眾**。

⑤ 如果你實在無法直接和部分聽眾做眼神接觸，那就看著他們的**鼻樑或下巴**，他們不會分辨出有什麼差別。

　　在做簡報時要記住上述六項重點，試著想像一下你希望以何種風格和口語表達方式呈現簡報內容。

3 Language style 語言風格

演說使用的語言會反映講者的風格，也會影響聽眾對於簡報的反應。好的簡報語言要清楚，並使人容易理解。

避免使用流行口號，這些一時流行且過度使用的口語詞彙意義並不明確。政治人物往往很喜歡使用這種流行口語，隱晦的意義讓他們的言詞缺乏可信度。

就語言風格而言，各種類型的慣用語，都可能讓外籍人士覺得難以理解，也難以使用，因為這些用語往往很陳舊、過時、不夠正式，或是屬於俚語，或不符演說風格。但就另一方面來看，**使用常用的片語動詞**能強化你的溝通技巧，它反映你近乎英語母語人士的語言能力，且不太容易說出錯誤的用語。

「**慣用語式片語動詞**」（idiomatic phrasal verb）和「**口語慣用語**」（idiomatic expression）不同，前者語言學家有時會直接稱作「**片語動詞**」（phrasal verb），兩者的差別在於片語動詞像「blow up」（爆炸）雖然屬於慣用語，但口語化的程度不及「blow your stack」（氣瘋了）這類口語慣用語。

一般的**片語動詞**結構為動詞後接一個副詞或介系詞，如「break down」；以「The workmen broke down the wall.」這句話為例，片語動詞 break down 的意義為「摧毀」。

不過 break down 作為慣用語，還有其他意義，以下例句列出了 break down 在句子中的不同意思。

❶ He **broke down** the theory.
他**分析**這個理論。

❷ The projector **broke down** during the presentation.
這部投影機在演說進行時**故障**了。

❸ When he heard about the bankruptcy, he **broke down**.
當他聽到破產的消息，他整個人**崩潰**了。

　　片語動詞若與名詞結合成詞組，有三種不同的用法，包括可分開的片語動詞、不可分開的片語動詞、或不及物片語動詞。

▶ **Separable** （可分開的片語動詞） ◖03◗

buy out 併購他人企業

❶ When we have enough capital, we will offer to **buy** them **out**.
等我們擁有足夠的資本，就會把它們**併購**下來。

❷ Microsoft has **bought out** Nokia.
微軟已**併購**諾基亞。

<table>
其他
範例
</table>

❶ **hand out** 分發
I'll **hand** the related information **out** later.
我晚點會將相關資訊**發給**大家。

❷ **leave out** 省略
Should we **leave** the last part **out**?
我們該**省略**最後一部分嗎？

❸ **spell out** 解釋
If you don't understand, I can **spell** it **out** for you.
若你不了解，我可以**解釋**給你聽。

❹ **try out** 測試
As for the new process, R&D will **try** it **out** to see if it cuts costs.
至於新的程序，研發部門會**測試**看看是否能節省開支。

❺ **wind up** 結束
I've only got a few minutes left, so I'll **wind** this **up** now.
我只剩幾分鐘了，我要開始**做結**。

count on 信賴;依靠

❶ You can **count on** my support.
你可以**信賴**我的幫助。

✕ You can **count** support **on** me.

其他範例

① **back out** 退出
The client can't **back out** from the deal because the contract is signed.
客戶無法**退出**這項交易,因為他們已簽訂合約。

② **call for** 要求
This strategy **calls for** total commitment from both parties.
這項策略**需要**雙方的全力配合。

③ **do away with** 消滅
This kind of innovation will **do away with** the former standard.
這項創新技術會將**打破**過去的水準。

④ **face up to** 承認
They'll **face up to** the mistake only if we mention it.
若我們提出來,他們也只能**承認**這個錯誤。

⑤ **go over** 複習
Let me **go over** the main points.
讓我**重述**一下要點。

Intransitive　不及物片語動詞

catch up 趕上；追上

1 When we secure the new customers, we will **catch up**.
待我們抓緊新的顧客，就可以迎頭**趕上**。

2 We will **catch up with** the industry leader next quarter.
下一季我們就可以**追平**業界龍頭。

✗ We will **catch up** the industry leader next quarter.

其他範例

1 **blow over** 消失
We should wait for the situation to **blow over** before we act.
我們先等情勢**已過**再行動。

2 **get around** 流通
Rumors **get around** faster than the facts do.
流言**流通**的速度比事實還快。

3 **get by** 負荷；勝任
Some members of the department are barely able to **get by**.
該部門的一些員工已經快不堪**負荷**了。

4 **make up** 和好
After the debt is paid, they should **make up** and become partners again.
等到債務還清後，他們應該**和好**並再度當合作夥伴。

5 **turn out** 參加
I'm happy that so many people have **turned out** for this event.
我很高興有這麼多人來**參加**此次盛會。

要增進口語式片語動詞的應用能力，最好的方法就是仔細研究介系詞或副詞在句中的位置。例如 play up 指強調，而 play down 則是弱化、輕描淡寫。

以下提供10組單字，它們在加上不同介系詞後會代表不同的意思。

① Go

① The orders have been confirmed, so delivery must **go on** as scheduled.

訂單已確認，因此商品必須照原定計畫**繼續進行**配送。

② That tie really **goes with** that shirt!

這條領帶與那件襯衫**好搭**！

③ They will probably **go along** with the plan if we include their input.

若我們將他們納入生產計畫，他們應該也會**同意依照**我們的計畫走。

④ Can we all **go in on** the taxi fee so it's affordable?

我們可以一起**分擔**計程車費好減輕費用負擔嗎？

② Come

① I'm here to report on how the overseas operation is **coming along**.

我來這裡報告海外營運的目前**狀況**。

② The new report **comes out** in the spring.

新的報告會在春季**出來**。

③ I **came by** this report in the library.

我是在圖書館**取得**這份報告的。

④ If this situation **comes up** again, let me know.

若此情況又再度**出現**，請通知我。

3 Get

① Even after his training in China, he barely **gets by**.

即使他已去中國受訓，他的表現只勉強**及格**而已。

② If we begin preparing now, we will **get through** the next week.

若我們現在就開始著手進行準備，我們下禮拜便能**順利完成**。

③ If they try to **get away with** overcharging again, we will cancel next year's deal.

若他們又設法**規避**索價過高的代價，我們將取消明年與他們的交易。

④ Since the merger, they haven't been able to **get along**.

自公司被併購後，他們就無法好好**相處**。

4 Take

① We will **take in** the sights as soon as there is a break in the meeting schedule.

一到會議休息時間時，我們會去**看**風景。

② Sales of the new product have really **taken off** recently.

新產品的銷售量近來不斷**提升**。

③ This budget proposal **takes after** the last one in too many ways.

此次的預算提案書**與**上次的有太多**相似**之處。

④ We want to **take on** as many people as we can for the job.

我們希望能盡量**僱用**員工來做此工作。

5 Make

① The people sitting in the back can't **make out** what the lecturer is saying.

坐在後面的人**聽不清楚**講者在說什麼。

② Next year's surplus should **make up** for this year's shortfall.

下一年的盈餘應該會**補償**今年的損失。

③ The building will be totally **made over** in order to increase its energy efficiency.

這棟建築物需要被徹底**整修**以成為節能建築。

④ We won't **make off with** any profit if we leave now.

若我們現在就離開是**無法得到**任何利益的。

6 Hold

① **Hold on** a minute, and I'll explain the process in more detail.

等我一分鐘,我會將整個流程做更仔細的解說。

② You might want to **hold off on** the order until next spring.

你也許可以考慮把這筆訂單**延到**明年春天。

③ He was **holding down** two jobs in order to pay his rent.

他以前**身兼**兩份工作以支付房租。

④ We can't afford to **hold out against** their offer much longer.

我們無法再繼續**拒絕**他們的提案了。

7 Put

① We'll **put** our guests **up** at the hotel during the conference.

在研討會期間，我們會將賓客**安置**在旅館。

② The new CEO doesn't **put up with** average performance.

新的執行長不能**忍受**普通的工作表現。

③ This improved production process **puts out** twice as many units as before.

這項改良過後的生產流程讓生產力**提升**兩倍。

④ If everyone can make it next week, we'll **put off** the final discussion until then.

若大家下個禮拜能來，我們就把最終討論**延**到那時。

⑧ Run

① If we **run across** the president, I'll introduce you to her.

若我們**碰見**總裁，我會把你介紹給她。

② I know you have an appointment, so the meeting won't **run on** past 3:00 p.m.

我知道你待會有事，所以會議不會**進行**超過下午三點。

③ The team should **run through** the steps one more time.

小組應該再**順**一次流程。

④ They **ran up** a large bill at the bar in just a few hours.

他們才在酒吧幾個小時就已**累積**了一筆高額帳單。

9 Look

① Peter's neighbor **looked after** his dog while he went on a business trip.

彼得的鄰居在他出差時幫他**照顧**他的狗。

② **Look out for** each other so no one gets hurt.

請彼此**關照**以避免任何人受傷。

③ You can **look up** the formula in the handout.

你可以在資料中**找到**公式。

④ Investors can **look forward to** better returns in the near future.

投資者可以**期盼**在不久後得到更好的投資報酬。

10 Play

① The chairman will **play down** the negative rumors about our position in the market.

董事長將會盡量**減少**對於我們在市場地位的不利傳言。

② In the next presentation, I'll **play up** the importance of the product's durability.

在下場簡報中，我會**著重**在此產品耐久的重要性。

③ We can **play with** the order of the presentations later.

我們之後可以再**調整**簡報內容的順序。

④ We can **play back** the recording if you want to hear it again.

若你想再重聽錄音內容，我們可以**重播**一次。

UNIT 6
Practicing the Presentation
簡報模擬練習

如果你只在簡報前五分鐘隨意瀏覽一下筆記就上台，那麼先前的細心準備就完全付諸流水了。事先預演幾次，能大大增進簡報的效果，你可以搭配相關器材練習，找出簡報裡所有重點細節，加進口頭簡報的內容後，就構成簡報最重要的最後步驟。

1. Know your equipment 熟悉簡報器材
2. Memorize the right stuff 記住正確的內容
3. Visualize your performance 將簡報視覺化
4. Work on your timing 時間的分配與掌控

1 Know your equipment 熟悉簡報器材

在簡報開始才摸索筆記型電腦或輔助器材的用法，是打壞聽眾第一印象的主因。關於筆記型電腦，請注意以下幾點：

❶ 暫停「自動關機」的功能。

❷ 學習如何使用電腦的紅外線遙控器。

❸ 把簡報的檔案放在電腦桌面，或是其他容易找到的位置。

至於其他視覺輔助器材，例如產品樣本，其黃金使用守則就是「**越簡單越好**」。太多視覺效果會讓你的簡報變得複雜。其他相關道具也是一樣，最簡單或容易操作的東西，往往能呈現最佳效果，例如管理學大師湯姆‧彼得斯（Tom Peters）就利用烹飪計時器，說明中國大陸工廠的擴展有多迅速。

但是還有另一項重點：簡報使用的道具，不能太可愛或太奇特。事實上，除非你是天生的幽默大師，不然最好別在簡報進行時搞笑，無論你是說笑話或使用讓人發噱的道具。

如果可能，最好能在實際做簡報的場所進行練習，找出照明燈具的位置；若你是在類似大禮堂的地方做簡報，則找到講台光亮的區域。

2 Memorize the right stuff 記住正確的內容

　　要記下整場簡報內容是不切實際的想法，但是如果能記得其中某些部分，其實對簡報很有幫助。有些專家建議背下**開頭五分鐘的每一句話和每一句手勢**，不但能加強效果，也能減輕緊張的程度。

　　除此之外，你也應該**記下簡報的重點**。逐字記下綱要的內容，或至少記住每個要點的正確說法，另外也需記憶一部分佐證的相關數據；但是大部分的事實資料，必須用**投影片**說明，或是採取更好的方法，像是提供**講義**給聽眾。

　　把大量數據資料呈現在聽眾面前，會讓觀眾感到枯燥乏味。別只是把數字塞進腦中，應該**將所有事實和特徵，轉化為具象化的優點和實際經驗**。

　　當史帝夫‧賈伯斯（Steve Jobs，蘋果公司的創辦人及前首席執行長）在介紹容量 30GB 的 iPod 時，並沒有預料到觀眾會對記憶體的容量感到訝異，這主要是因為他以 30GB 代表 7,500 首歌、25,000 張圖片或 75 小時長度的影片，詳細並具像地說明了產品規格。

▲Steve Jobs

3 Visualize your performance 將簡報視覺化

　　當你認為所有投影片已經製作完美，而你也已經熟記所有簡報的綱要，即可以實際演練一次。**將預演狀況錄製下來**是個很好的方法，可以從影像得到立即的回應。

　　開啟 PowerPoint 開始做簡報，說出仔細研究過的所有台詞、實際操作設想過的所有動作；做完簡報演練後觀看影片檔，評論一下自己的表現，根據簡報的**引言**、**主要內容**和**表達方式**，用下列問題自我檢測，找出可以改進的目標。在此階段，你可以再瀏覽最早開始進行簡報的重點問題，確保你沒有偏離原本的簡報目標。

❶	Introduction 引言	• 你的開場白夠引人入勝嗎、主題夠清楚嗎？ • 有沒有涵蓋整場簡報的內容結構？
❷	Content 主要內容	• 你是否每一個分項要點都介紹得清楚完整，才進入下一個新的主題？ • 你的論點結構是否具備邏輯性？ • 你提供的事實資料是否精確？ • 投影片的內容容易理解嗎？ • 當你下結論時，是否已經將引言中引導的部分說明清楚？簡報的內容和聽眾是否直接相關？
❸	Conclusion 結論	• 你的簡報主題是否已經有效地傳達給聽眾？ • 簡報的收尾是否也和開頭一樣具說服力？
❹	Delivery 表達能力	• 在做簡報時，你的表情是否夠放鬆？是否具備熱忱？ • 你的行為或肢體語言是否流露緊張感？ • 你的手勢動作是否強化或減弱訊息的傳遞？ • 簡報的用詞有沒有重複？ • 你的聲音會不會太大或太小？音量會不會小得像在喃喃自語？說話速度會不會太快？ • 你有說明解釋投影片的內容，或是一字不漏地將投影片上的文字唸出來？ • 你是否有技巧地運用各種工具？ • 身為簡報的主角，你有沒有吸引聽眾注意？或是讓他們覺得無趣？

4 Work on your timing　時間的分配與掌控

最後一項評斷自己表現的標準是**對時間的掌控**，一場簡報的時間應該分配如下：

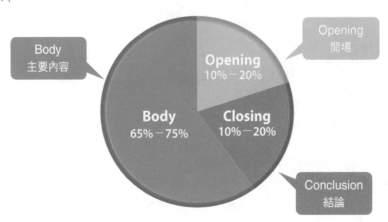

除此之外，在簡報當天你說話的速度可能因為緊張而加快，而實際的簡報時間，也可能因為觀眾在好奇之下詢問了更多問題，而較預估的時間更久。

PART 2

PHRASES FOR PRE-INTRODUCTION SMALL TALK

開場白之前的閒談

在做小型簡報時，往往因為聽眾遲到或是器材的問題，在進入簡報主題前，會有一小段時間能和觀眾做比較隨性的接觸。在這種情況下，和他們握手寒暄、閒聊一會兒，或是彼此交換名片都是合宜的作法。

UNIT 7
Casual Introductions and Small Talk
自我介紹及閒談

UNIT 7
Casual Introductions and Small Talk
自我介紹及閒談

開場白前的閒談能藉由互動，拉近你與觀眾的距離，也讓你有機會認識他們，對簡報有極大助益。

1. Casual Introductions 自我介紹
2. Small Talk 閒談

1 Casual Introductions 自我介紹

　　雖然每個場合的情況會有些許不同，但一般來說，自我介紹的口氣只要表現出友善、隨性、熱忱即可。

① Hi, I'm John. Nice to meet you.
　你好，我是約翰。很高興認識你。

② Hello, I'm John Smith. It's a pleasure to be here.
　你好，我是約翰‧史密斯，很高興來到這裡。

③ John Smith. Hello!
　我是約翰‧史密斯。你好！

④ How're you doing? I'm John.
　你好嗎？我叫約翰。

2 Small Talk 閒談

　　閒談就是針對一般人有興趣的主題隨意交談，適合閒聊的主題會因為文化、政治環境和其他因素而有所不同。如果你對聽眾有一定的了解，就應該知道哪些是最好且最適當的話題，而跨文化最安全的話題就是**聊天氣**。

① Weather 聊天氣

① So is it always this rainy this time of year?
所以這裡每年到這時候都一直下雨嗎？

② Is this normal weather for this time of year?
每年此時天氣都是這樣嗎？

③ Sure is hot today!
今天的確很熱！

④ What a beautiful morning!
真是個美好的早晨啊！

⑤ The weather sure changed quickly this afternoon!
今天下午天氣變得實在太快了！

⑥ Couldn't have asked for a better day!
天氣好得不能再好了！

② Travel 聊旅遊

↳ 旅遊也是很容易聊開的話題

① You've been to Palau? I was there last year. It's amazing!
你去過帛琉？我去年也在那裡，真神奇！

② I arrived last night from LA. I'm still feeling a little jet-lagged actually.
我昨晚從洛杉磯過來，其實現在還有一點時差。

③ I haven't been to Japan yet; what's it like?
我還沒去過日本，那裡的景色怎麼樣？

③ Mutual Friends and Places 聊共同認識的人事物

↳ 共同的朋友、學校或公司都是很不錯的話題

① You know Jack? What a coincidence! I worked with him about six years ago.
你認識傑克？真是太巧了！我六年前和他共事過呢。

② I heard you studied at NTU. Small world! I studied there, too!
聽說你是台大畢業的，世界真小！我也在那裡念書。

③ I worked for TSMC for a short time, too.
我也在台積電工作過一小段時間。

④ Cultural Differences 聊文化的不同

↳ 要注意的是只可比較不可批評

① I tried the dumplings, and let me tell you, they are totally different from what they sell in the United States.
我吃過這兒的水餃了，和美國賣的完全不同。

② Vegetarian? Me? Not really by your definition. I don't eat meat, but I do eat onions and garlic.
吃素？我嗎？根據你對素食的定義我應該不算。雖然我不吃肉，不過我還是吃洋蔥和大蒜。

③ The traffic here is comparable to the traffic in Los Angeles, for sure.
這裡的交通絕對可以和洛杉磯當地相比。

69

Scenario 模擬情境

Imagine that you're meeting with a member of the audience who will be attending your presentation in a few hours. The meeting is taking place in a Starbucks coffee shop in Karachi, Pakistan.

假設你在幾小時後要舉辦一場演講，地點在巴基斯坦喀拉蚩的星巴克，此時你遇見一位即將參加你演講的聽眾。

The Audience 簡報對象

The man you're meeting is a procurement manager for the company where you are presenting today. You are selling IT hardware. You have never met this man before.

You see that he is young and sharply dressed, with a taste for the latest European fashion trends. So far, he has been quick-witted but a little long-winded and loud. He has a strong Hindi accent, but his English is fluent. He wears a Bluetooth headset and a watch that costs more than the car you drive back home. He wears a diamond-studded peace symbol on a silver chain around his neck. He's carrying a notebook. It's a MacBook Air. He has a flaming electric guitar, snakes, and skulls tattooed on his right forearm. He orders a black coffee with three additional espresso shots—no cream, no sugar.

Your background check wasn't very fruitful, so all you have to go on are these first impressions.

這位對象是今日進行簡報公司的採購經理，你要向他們販售IT硬體，你和採購經理今天是初次見面。

他很年輕，穿衣風格符合目前歐洲最新潮流，從對話中聽得出他頗機智，但是有些囉嗦且嗓門很大；他的印度腔很重，不過英文說得很流利。他戴著藍牙耳機，手錶的價值比你開的車還貴重，脖子上戴的是鑽石銀鍊，上面鑲嵌代表和平的標誌。他的筆電是 MacBook Air，他右前臂上有刺青，圖形分別是燃燒的電吉他、蛇和骷髏。他點的飲料是黑咖啡外加三份濃縮咖啡，不加糖和奶精。

你對他的背景所知不多，所以只能靠這些第一印象展開聊天話題。

✓ Appropriate Topics for Small Talk 適合的閒聊主題

- What's playing on his mobile phone
  他手機裡的歌
- His childhood home
  童年的家
- Bungee jumping
  高空彈跳
- The last book you read
  你最近讀的書
- The local sports team
  當地的運動隊伍
- Learning a language
  學習新語言
- Hotspot connectivity
  熱點連線

- Open source software
  自由軟體
- His fashionable clothes
  他的時尚打扮
- Keeping healthy
  養生
- Your current job
  你目前的工作
- Your last vacation
  你的上個假期
- A recent environmental disaster in the area
  近來該區的天災
- Rock and roll
  搖滾樂

✗ Inappropriate Topics for Small Talk 不適合的閒聊主題

- Recent Bollywood movies
  最近的寶萊塢電影
- Your divorce
  你的離婚
- Capital punishment
  死刑
- Your annual income
  你的年收入
- The war on terror
  打擊恐怖分子
- Your favorite actor
  你最愛的影星
- Sleep disorders and caffeine addiction
  睡眠障礙與咖啡因上癮
- Gardening
  園藝
- Political party
  政黨

- Religion
  宗教
- Global warming
  全球暖化
- Your health problems
  你的健康問題
- Your family
  你的家人
- Popular magazines
  熱門雜誌
- A nearby tourist attraction
  附近的熱門景點
- Human cloning
  複製人
- Finding a job in your country
  找工作

PART **3**

PHRASES FOR PRESENTING THE INTRODUCTION

簡報開場白的用語

第一印象雖然很重要，但在做自我介紹時請別忘了一個重點——簡報的主角不是你，你的目的是要把主題內容介紹給聽眾。所以自我介紹應該簡短單純，並能流暢地引導聽眾進入簡報的內容。

 UNIT 8 Introducing Yourself
自我介紹

 UNIT 9 Introducing the Subject
介紹簡報主題

Introducing Yourself
自我介紹

好的自我介紹能讓聽眾認識你、了解簡報背景並立刻進入狀況。

等所有聽眾的注意力都在你身上後，才開始自我介紹。以最簡單的「早安」或「午安」起頭，展現自信心與輕鬆的態度。

簡單介紹一下自己，如有必要，在介紹名字時直接加上在公司的正式職稱。如果你不是當地人，也簡單說明一下自己來自哪裡，同時說明簡報的主題。

① **Good morning. My name is** Tina Gonzales. **I'm** a sales rep with Acme Server Technology in California, **and I'm here today to talk about** the latest Acme technology and what it can do for your company.

早安，我是蒂娜‧岡薩里斯，加州尖端科技公司的業務代表，**今天我來到這裡，是要向各位說明**敝公司最新的發展，以及我們能為貴公司所提供的服務。

② **Good morning. I'm delighted to be here today. My name is** Natas Kamps. **I'm here** from Document Outsourcing Solutions to **discuss** how our services work and the benefits for your company.

早安！很開心今天來到這裡。我是納塔斯‧喀布斯，**我代表**文件外包顧問公司和各位**談談**我們所提供的服務事項，以及貴公司能得益的部分。

③ **Good morning, ladies and gentlemen. Thanks for having me here today.** I'm Annie Templeton of Mainstring Marketing. As you know, I'm here to present our company profile.

女士先生們，早安！非常謝謝各位邀請我來，我是主線行銷公司的安妮‧坦普頓。相信各位都知道，今天我來的目的是要向各位介紹我的公司。

④ **Good morning**. **Let me introduce myself**. **I'm** Chris Shao, **representing** HAL A.I. and Robotics. **My** talk today is about our latest technology and its potential for your future.

早安！**請容我先自我介紹一下**。**我是**克里斯・邵，**代表**海爾人工智慧暨機械研發公司。今天**我的**演說是有關本公司的最新科技，以及它對您的未來有哪些潛在的幫助。

⑤ **Good morning**. **Welcome and thank you for coming**. **I'm** Debra Dreble, and today I'll be presenting some ideas about lowering costs in the workplace.

早安！**歡迎並感謝您今天的參與**。**我是**黛布拉・德瑞伯。今天我要報告的內容是關於減低工作場所成本的一些建議方法。

如果**你的名字很特別或不容易發音，則放慢速度**，清楚地對觀眾說出自己的姓名。簡報投影片的標題頁上，應該註明簡報人姓名，在做自我介紹時同時播放該頁投影片。

UNIT 9 Introducing the Subject
介紹簡報主題

介紹簡報時，引言（the hook）、主旨（the thesis）和簡報概要（the overview）三個部分是不可或缺的。

1. The hook 引言
2. The thesis 主旨
3. The overview 簡報概要
4. Signaling the end of the introduction and the beginning of the content
   為介紹做結，進入主要內容

1 The hook 引言

引言內容應該與**事實資料**密切相關，要以聽眾具備的背景知識吸引聽眾對簡報內容產生興趣。引言的主要目的，是別讓聽眾一邊聽你的簡介一邊想「……那又如何？」，同時也**要為簡報主題建構基礎**。

引言可能有以下幾種不同的模式。

① Thought-provoking and relevant questions
提出一個激發聽眾興趣的相關問題，之後在進行簡報時回答。

① **Have you ever wondered what it would be like** to increase data retrieval, security, and the overall performance of your company's network?

你是否曾經想過，改善你電腦網路取得資料的功能、安全性以及整體運作效能後**會有什麼不同**？

② **What if** outsourcing of your technical manual could improve the quality of the writing and lower its cost?

如果將撰寫操作手冊的工作外包能改善品質又能降低成本呢？

③ **Ask yourself**, is your in-house marketing department as effective as it could be?

問問自己，公司編制內的行銷部門真有達到預期的成果嗎？

④ **Consider for a moment**, exactly what is it that separates your assembly line's efficiency from the world's best?

請思考一下，究竟是什麼因素使你們公司的裝配線產能與世界最佳的產能越差越多？

⑤ **Would you like to** find the ultimate solution for reducing your company's overhead?

你希望找出降低公司成本的絕佳方法嗎？

② A brief story
一則能引發聽眾切身感受的小故事，並藉此導引至簡報正題。

① **Last month, I was in New York chatting with** a network administrator about server uptime. **He told me that** network disruptions were costing him an amazing amount of money.

上個月，我在紐約和一位網路行政人員聊到主機的正常運作時間，他告訴我因為網路連線中斷，讓他耗費了大量的成本。

② **While in Taipei last month, I was having lunch with** the project manager of a well-known computer company. **She was complaining about how** technical documentation was never finished on time.

上個月我在台北與一家知名電腦公司的專案管理經理共進午餐，她向我抱怨技術文件從來沒有準時完成過。

③ **A few weeks ago, I was at a trade show in Dubai with** Elsa Steamer from sales. **She explained to me** that the company's in-house marketing will be handled by a consultant from now on.

幾週前我和業務部門的伊莉莎‧史丁默一起**參加杜拜的貿易展**。她告訴我從現在起,公司的內部行銷將會交給一位顧問管理。

④ **I'm reminded of my visit to Seoul last month. While touring the plant there, I ran into** Justin Stranger from production. **He was telling me** that a new car rolls off the assembly line in Korea every 57 seconds.

這讓我想起了上個月到首爾的情形。在參觀工廠的時候我遇到了賈斯丁‧史崔哲,**他告訴我**在韓國每 57 秒就有一台新車在裝配線上組好。

⑤ **I was in Montreal last month on business, and I ran into** Rick Crank. **He** is running logistics now and **let me know that** since the company sublet the fourth floor, overhead has been reduced by 30 percent!

上個月我到蒙特婁出差遇到瑞克‧克蘭,他目前負責管理產品物流。**他告訴我**自從公司將四樓轉租後,成本已經減少了 30%。

2 The thesis 主旨

　　主旨就是簡報的核心，或是簡報的中心論點。簡報主旨應該**直接明瞭**，反映簡報的整體內容，同時也包含提供給簡報對象的機會與利益。

① The server technology **I'm talking about today** will improve your network's efficiency by reducing system downtime.

今天我提到的伺服器端科技，能夠藉由減低系統停機時間來增進網路效能。

② **I'm going to show that** outsourcing your technical documentation saves time, lowers cost, and improves quality.

現在我要展示的是，將技術文件外發能夠節省時間、降低成本，以及改善品質。

③ **I want you to understand how** our expertise in marketing can make your brand more recognizable to consumers.

希望各位能夠了解，我們在行銷的專業，能讓顧客對貴公司的品牌更熟悉。

④ **What I'm saying is that** the hands-on approach could be more reliable and could yield better quality control than a totally automated system.

我的意思是，手動操作較為可靠，產品的品質也會比全自動系統生產的更好。

⑤ **My point is** that overhead can be reduced and funds can be reinvested more productively.

我的重點是，可以減少間接成本並再投資資金以獲取更大的生產效益。

3 The overview 簡報概要

簡報概要是讓聽眾對**簡報的流程**有概略的了解，知道接下來會介紹哪些內容。它讓報告的內容更具體，而你講述的一切也變得更有意義。

① **I will introduce** the latest server platform technology and then describe each component of the platform in turn. **I will show** exactly how each component will improve your company's efficiency, and **I will conclude with a comparison between** Acme's server technology and its competitors' server technologies.

我會向各位介紹最新穎的伺服器平台科技，並依序說明構成該平台的每一項要件。**我會展示**每一個要件會如何增進貴公司的效能，**最後以比較**尖端伺服器端科技公司及其競爭對手的伺服器端科技**作為總結**。

② **I will begin with** some examples of documentation that has been improved upon by our team. **Then I will demonstrate** our research methods and documentation SOP. **Finally**, **I will compare** the processes and costs of outsourced documentation with those of full-time staff.

首先我會提供一些由我們團隊改善過的技術文件範例，**接著示範**我們的研究方法及技術文件的標準作業流程，**最後我會比較**將文件工作外包和由全職員工進行的流程和成本。

③ **First, I will outline** some relevant trends in modern marketing. **Next, I will clarify** exactly how our focus groups can determine the goals for your company's network efficiency and reliability. **In conclusion, I will point out the differences between** successful and unsuccessful marketing campaigns.

首先我會概述目前市場的相關趨勢，**接著詳細說明**我們的聚焦小組如何能為貴公司的網路效能和信賴度設定目標，**最後，我會指出**成功和失敗的行銷活動**之間的差異**。

④ **I'll start off by taking a look at** the history of assembly line automation. Then, I'll **go on to highlight** the terms used for defining reliability and quality control. **Lastly, I'll lay out the arguments for and against** totally automated systems.

我首先會帶各位認識裝配線自動化的歷史進程，**接著會著重在**可信度和品質管理等專有名詞的定義，**最後，我會提出贊成與反對**全自動化系統兩方的論點來做結。

⑤ **I'll begin by bringing you up-to-date** on recent changes to our total overhead reduction plan. **I will also show** how savings can be redistributed for maximum returns. **At the end**, **I'll describe a before-and-after scenario** that illustrates the long-term benefits of this solution.

一開始我會先向各位介紹近來我們為降低總經費所提出的最新改變計畫，**同時說明**如何重新分配存款以獲取最大的報酬。**最後，我將解說採取此方式前後的情況**以說明長期執行此方案的好處。

A Introducing a New Solution 介紹新方案

Hi, I'm Mina Koston. It's a pleasure to be here. **self introduction**

You know, when I think about documentation outsourcing, I'm reminded of last month, when I was having lunch with the project manager of a well-known computer company. She was complaining about how technical documentation was never finished on time. **hook**

The fact is, a lot of companies are faced with this dilemma. Today, I want to explain how outsourcing your technical documentation saves time, lowers cost, and improves quality. **thesis**

I will begin with some examples of when documentation has been improved upon by our team of writers. Then, I will demonstrate our research methods and documentation SOP. Finally, I will compare the processes and costs of outsourced documentation with those of full-time in-house staff. **overview**

嗨，我是米娜・柯斯頓，很高興來到這裡。當我想到將技術文件外包這件事，我就想到上個月，我與一位知名電腦公司專案經理的午餐之約。當時，她向我抱怨技術文件的製作總是無法在時限前完成。事實上，許多公司都有同樣的狀況。今天我將要解釋，將技術文件外包不但省時、省預算，也能提升品質。我將先舉幾個例子，說明敝公司的員工是如何改善文件的品質；接著，我將示範研究方法和作業流程；最後我將比較將文件工作外包和由全職員工進行的流程和成本。

B　Branding 建立品牌形象

Hello. I'm Lance Marton with Better Business Marketing. I'm here to talk about our brand-building expertise and new services.　**self introduction**

I'd like you to consider this question for a moment: Is your in-house marketing department as effective as it could be?　**hook**

My goal today is to show how our expertise in marketing can make your brand more recognizable to consumers.　**thesis**

First, I will outline some relevant trends in modern marketing. Next, I will clarify exactly how our focus groups can define your company's brand image. In conclusion, I will point out the differences between successful and unsuccessful marketing campaigns.　**overview**

哈囉，我是向榮行銷公司的藍斯·茂頓，我來這裡介紹敝公司建立品牌形象的專業和新服務。我想請你們思考一下這個問題，您是否滿意貴公司的行銷部的效率？我今日的目標，是向您展示我們在行銷方面的專業長才，這將能讓消費者對貴公司的品牌更加熟悉。首先，我將列出目前市場的相關潮流；接著，我將清楚解釋我們的聚焦小組是如何決定貴公司的品牌形象。最後，我會指出成功和失敗的行銷活動之間的差異。

C Cutting Costs 節省預算

Good afternoon, everyone, I'm Bob Burn, and I'm here today to present some ideas about downsizing. Would you like to find another solution for reducing your company's overhead? The main point I want to deliver today is that with our proven techniques, overhead can be reduced and funds can be reinvested more productively. I'll begin by bringing you up-to-date on recent changes to our total overhead reduction plan. I will also show how savings can be redistributed for maximum returns. At the end, I'll describe a before-and-after scenario that illustrates the long-term benefits of this solution.

self introduction

hook

thesis

overview

大家午安,我是鮑伯・伯恩,我今天要向你們呈現一些與縮編相關的想法。你們想找另一種減少公司間接成本的方式嗎?我今日的演講重點是,只要採用敝公司幾經試驗成功的方式,將能減少間接成本,讓資金能再被投資,產生效益。我將介紹我們近來採取的降低總間接成本計畫,我也將說明要如何再重新分配存款以獲得最大的報酬。最後,我將解說採取此方式前後的情況以說明長期執行此方案的好處。

4 Signaling the end of the introduction and the beginning of the content 為介紹做結，進入主要內容

① **So that concludes the introduction**. I'll move on now to a more-detailed description of the main points of my presentation.

以上就是我對主題的介紹，接著我會清楚説明簡報的幾項重點。

② **OK. Now I'll describe** my main points in more detail.

好的，**現在我會**更仔細地**解說**我提出的各個要點。

③ **OK then. The next section** goes into greater detail on the subject.

好，我在**下一個階段**會更深入説明主題的內容。

PART 4

PHRASES FOR PRESENTING THE CONTENT
闡明簡報主題的用語

本單元旨在闡述簡報主要內容的慣用語，這些慣用語會根據其常用於簡報中的16種溝通模式分類。

Indicating Your Preference for Dealing With Questions
表達處理聽眾提問的方式

關於如何回應聽眾的問題，你可以在簡報一開始時說明。

1. Taking questions at the end 簡報結束時回答問題
2. Taking questions at any time 簡報進行中任一時間點回答問題

1 Taking questions at the end 簡報結束時回答問題

在較大的場地做簡報時，最好是簡報結束再回答問題。

① I'll answer questions at the end of the presentation.
我會在簡報最後回答大家的問題。

② I'll deal with questions at the end of the presentation.
我會在簡報結束時處理各位的問題。

③ I'll take questions at the end of the presentation.
在簡報最後我會讓大家提問。

④ I'll open the floor to questions at the end of the presentation.
簡報結束後我會開放讓各位發問。

2 Taking questions at any time
簡報進行中任一時間點回答問題

　　如果你是在比較小的場地做簡報，堅持到簡報結束才願意回答問題就顯得不太恰當，甚至有些無禮。你可以對聽眾說明，隨時都很歡迎他們提問。

① Please don't hesitate to interrupt me at any time if you have a question or comment.

　　若你有任何疑問或意見，可以隨時向我提問。

② Feel free to stop me whenever you like if you have a question or comment.

　　如果你有任何問題或是意見，可以直接告訴我，不用擔心打斷我做簡報。

③ Please don't think twice about jumping in at any time with any questions you have.

　　若是你有任何疑問，不必遲疑，隨時可以打斷我。

　　如何在簡報進行中或結束後回應聽眾的問題，在本書 PART 5 中最後會有更詳細的說明。

UNIT 11 Distributing Handouts
資料發送方式

你必須在簡報進行時，對聽眾解釋將如何分發講義。

1. Distributing your handout at the beginning 簡報一開始就發送文字資料
2. Distributing your handout at the end 在簡報結束時發送文字資料
3. Distributing your handout via email 用電子郵件發送文字資料

1 Distributing your handout at the beginning
簡報一開始就發送文字資料

在簡報一開始就將資料發給聽眾的好處是，他們能直接在紙張上做筆記（take notes）。

★ 如果這些資料是由**你自行發給聽眾**，你可以說：

① The handouts I'm passing out now have all the supplemental information you'll need.

我現在發的資料裡有你需要的所有補充資訊。

★ 如果你的資料**先前已經發給聽眾了**，你可以說：

② Has everyone gotten a copy of my handout? It has all the slides I'll be showing today, space for taking notes, and appendixes at the back for your reference later.

每個人都拿到我提供的資料了嗎？裡面包含了所有我今天要播放的投影片內容。上面有空間可以做筆記，背面的附錄可讓你們稍後做參考。

★ **配合當場的情況**，你也可以說：

③ I hope everyone has a copy of the handout.

希望每個人都有拿到一份資料。

④ I trust everyone received the handout.

相信各位都已經拿到資料了。

2 Distributing your handout at the end
在簡報結束時發送文字資料

⑤ Don't worry about taking notes. I'll give you the slides in a handout at the end of the presentation.

你們不用做筆記,簡報結束後我會發放文字資料給各位,裡面包含了投影片的內容。

⑥ All the slides in my presentation today are in the handout. I'll give that to you later.

今天簡報的投影片內容全在資料內,我之後會發給各位。

3 Distributing your handout via email
用電子郵件發送文字資料

⑦ You needn't bother copying the information on the slides. I'll email the PowerPoint file to all of you.

不必抄寫投影片上的資訊,我會把投影片檔案用電子郵件傳給你們。

⑧ If you leave your email address with me at the end of the presentation, I'll send the PowerPoint file to you.

若你們在簡報結束後把電子郵件地址留下來,我會把投影片檔案寄給你們。

Scenario 模擬情境

At a large venue with a question-and-answer period at the end and handouts distributed at the beginning

在較大的場地進行簡報，會後有提問時間；資料在簡報開始時就提供給聽眾了

Policy 處理方式

If you have any questions, I'll be happy to answer them during the Q&A session at the end. Handouts with all the relevant information were distributed at the door, so you should have everything you need. Please email me if you require additional information.

如果您有任何問題，我很樂意在簡報結束後的提問時間為您解答。相關的文字資料已在入口處發送，相信您已拿到所有的資料了。如果還需要其他資料，請來信通知。

Scenario 模擬情境

In a smaller venue where questions are welcome at any time and handouts are distributed throughout the presentation as needed

在較小的場地進行簡報，隨時都歡迎提問；資料會隨著簡報需要時才提供給聽眾

Policy 處理方式

Don't think twice about stopping me at any time if you have any questions or comments. Later, I'll be passing around some information that you'll find useful for future reference.

如果您在簡報進行時有任何問題或評論，請隨時提問。待會兒我會提供簡報相關資料給各位參考。

Scenario 模擬情境

In a large venue with a question-and-answer period and handout distribution at the end

在較大的場地進行簡報，會後有提問時間；資料在簡報尾聲時才會提供給聽眾

Policy 處理方式

I'll deal with questions at the end of the presentation if you don't mind. Don't worry about taking notes. I'll give you the slides in a handout at the end of the presentation.

如果各位不介意，我會在簡報的最後回答大家的問題。不用急著抄寫筆記，我在最後會提供投影片的文字資料。

UNIT 12

Introducing and Explaining Charts, Graphs, and Pictures
介紹並說明圖表

圖表和圖片（charts, graphs, and pictures）上顯示的原始數據資料（raw data）必須是淺顯易懂的。但為了確保他們接收的資訊正確無誤，講者必須說明當中數據代表的意義及其重要性。

1. Introducing a chart or graph 介紹表格或圖表
2. Explaining significant parts of charts and graphs 解釋圖表各部分的意義
3. Describing a picture 詳述圖片內容

---

1 Introducing a chart or graph 介紹表格或圖表

介紹圖表的目的是**讓聽眾轉移視覺焦點**，並且以常見的專門術語對他們說明圖表內容。

★ 介紹產品線

Big Momma's Gadgetry

Tablets 平板電腦　　PCs 桌上型電腦　　Notebooks 筆記型電腦

① **Take a look** at the company's current product lines.
請**看一下**該公司目前的產品線。

② **Here are** the product lines that the company is currently **focusing on**.
這些是該公司目前**主打的**產品線。

③ **Let's turn our attention to** the company's three current product lines.
現在讓我們來看這間公司目前的三條產品線。

★ 介紹產品線的銷售額

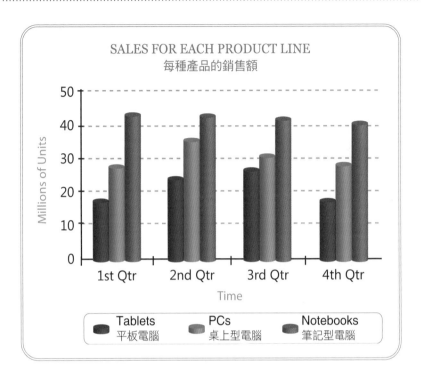

④ **As you can see from** this bar graph, the relative level of sales among the three lines was consistent in the first and fourth quarters.

從這個長條圖**可以看出**，這三項產品的相對銷售水準，在第一和第四季都維持很穩定的狀態。

⑤ **Looking at this** bar graph, **you'll see** the sales levels of the three lines were relatively consistent in the first and fourth quarters.

注意看這個長條圖，**你會發現**這三項產品的相對銷售水準，在第一和第四季維持很穩定的狀態。

⑥ **This** bar graph **shows** the consistency of sales for our three product lines, relative to each other, in the first and fourth quarters.

由長條圖的數據**顯示**，我們三條產品線的業績，在第一和第四季呈現穩定的相對關係。

2 Explaining significant parts of charts and graphs
解釋圖表各部分的意義

　　解釋圖表各部分定義時，也說明了視覺輔助資料所提供的事實、數據或專門術語。解釋內容主要由兩部分組成：**說明圖表內容**及**根據資料做出評析**。

★ 說明圖表內容

 說明 XY 軸各代表的意義

① **The horizontal axis represents** the sales quarters.
The vertical axis shows millions of units sold.

水平軸表示每一季的發展，**垂直軸表示**銷售數量，以百萬為單位。

② The axes are referred to as *x* and *y*:
The *y-axis* portrays . . .
The *x-axis* illustrates . . .

以軸線表示 X 軸和 Y 軸：Y 軸表示……X 軸代表……

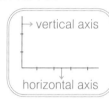

vertical axis

horizontal axis

 bar graph 說明長條圖

常用單字：row（列）、column（欄）和 legend（圖例說明）

③ As you can see, the blue **column** in the third quarter—representing East—was the high point of the year.

正如各位所見，第三季中代表東部地區的藍色**長條**，是一年當中的最高點。

④ Each region is identified by a different color, as you can see in the **legend**.

不同顏色代表不同地區，這點可以從**圖例**說明看出。

line graph 說明折線圖

常用單字：dotted line（虛線）、broken line（折線）、solid line（實線）

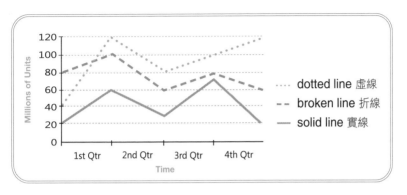

⑤ Let's talk about 2021 first, represented here by the solid blue line.

我們首先討論 2021 年的走勢，這裡是以藍色的實線代表。

 pie chart 說明圓餅圖

常用單字：segment（扇形）

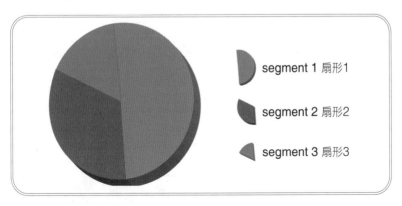

⑥ The blue segment represents families that own more than three cars.

藍色扇形的部分代表擁有三輛車以上的家庭。

針對圖表做進一步分析時，你可以一次說明其中一個部分。就已說明的圖表項目做評論，則圖表中的事實和數據就會轉化為實質的內容。

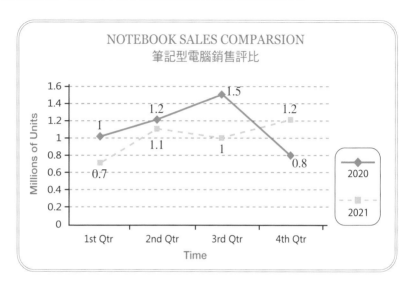

⑦ The first part of 2020 was marked by steady growth, with a disastrous slide in the fourth quarter, as we all know.

2020 年前期呈現穩定成長，而正如我們都知道的，第四季出現劇烈下滑。

以下範例是根據上一頁「筆記型電腦銷售評比」折線圖的內容，所撰寫的說明及評論：

Identification 說明	Commentary 評論
1 2020 was marked by steady growth; and, as we all know, a disastrous slide in the fourth quarter. 2020 年前期呈現穩定成長，而正如我們都知道的，第四季出現劇烈下滑。	This figure is not a fluke. Given similar market conditions, we can achieve steady growth again and hopefully sustain it. 這項數據並不是僥倖獲得，在類似的市場環境下，我們可以再次達成目標，也希望能夠維持下去。
2 Note the sharp decline to 0.8 million units during the fourth quarter of 2020. 請注意觀察，2020 第四季的銷售數量急遽下滑至 80 萬台。	The thing to remember here is that this drop was industrywide and probably won't happen again. 各位要注意的是，這一季整個業界的銷售量普遍下滑，未來應該不會再發生同樣的狀況。
3 Look at the sudden rise between the first and second quarters of 2021. 請看 2021 年第一季和第二季間，銷售數量呈現劇烈上升。	This rise was partly due to our major competitor pulling out of the European market. 這段時間銷售量攀升的原因是我們的主要競爭對手退出歐洲市場。
4 Think about the overall increase from 1 million to 1.2 million between the first quarter of 2020 and the fourth quarter of 2021. 2020 年第一季至 2021 年第四季間，總體銷售量從 100 萬增加至 120 萬台。	In the big picture, sales are improving—despite the emerging competition and last year's slip. 長期看來，即使面臨新興企業的競爭，以及去年的數字下滑，業績一直在進步。

Let's take a look at this graph showing increasing shipments for 2021. The steady rise in shipments reflects orders from our new customers, primarily the big account in China.

　讓我們看看這張圖表，它顯示我們 2021 年的出貨量不斷增加，表示這整年我們的客戶量是持續上升的。這要歸因於取得中國的重要客戶。

EXAMPLE B

Take a look at this diagram, which illustrates the shipping routes for our products. You can see that everything radiates out from the Taipei main warehouse. Therefore, the most logical location for our headquarters is the main warehouse.

這張圖表呈現出我們產品的運送路線，如圖中所示，所有的產品都由台北總倉庫送出，因此最合適的總部地點就是總倉庫。

Retail
Outlets
零售店

Taichung/Kaohsiung
台中/高雄

Taipei main warehouse
台北總倉庫

I want to turn now to this diagram depicting product stock quantities. Look at the middle layer, representing the local warehouses. It's important to note this layer's size. The warehouses are too full.

讓我們來看這張圖，它顯示出商品的存貨數量。金字塔中間那層是本地的倉庫，這層所佔的體積很重要，它表示倉庫的庫存量都太滿了。

EXAMPLE ⓓ

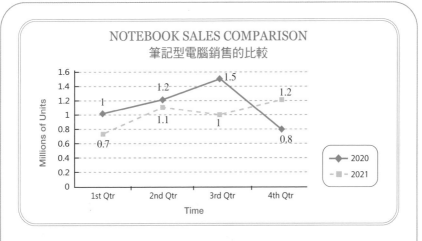

NOTEBOOK SALES COMPARISON
筆記型電腦銷售的比較

(Line chart: Y-axis "Millions of Units" 0 to 1.6; X-axis "Time" showing 1st Qtr, 2nd Qtr, 3rd Qtr, 4th Qtr. 2020 values: 1, 1.2, 1.5, 0.8. 2021 values: 0.7, 1.1, 1, 1.2. Legend: 2020, 2021)

❶ Decreased sales in the third quarter of 2014 were the result of an industrywide drop in consumer spending.

❷ Sales increased in the first quarter of 2014 because a major competitor pulled out of the market.

Notice the rise in sales during the second quarter of 2020. We believe this was related to the continued popularity of the embedded webcam. Another notable point was the fall in sales during the second quarter of 2021, the result of an industrywide decrease in consumer spending. The big turnaround in sales occurred between Q4 2020 and Q1 2021, when a major competitor pulled out of the market.

注意2020年第二季銷售量的增加，我們相信這與嵌入式視訊攝影機的流行有關。另一處值得注意的重點是 2021 年第二季降低的銷售量，這是由於本產業消費指數的下降。銷售量在 2020 年第四季和 2021 年第一季出現了轉折，這是由於一位主要競爭對手退出市場的緣故。

3 Describing a picture 詳述圖片內容

描述圖片的方式和說明圖表的方式其實沒有太大的差別：**向聽眾介紹圖片、針對重要部分說明**，最後做**重點評論**。

① This picture shows damage to the levee from the flood. In the lower right corner of the picture, you can see very clear evidence that the levee is extremely weak. If it keeps raining, the levee is going to break.

這張圖片呈現洪水對堤防造成的損害。圖片的右下角可以明顯看出堤防非常不牢固，如果大雨持續不停，堤防就會崩塌。

② Here you can see the new site for the hotel. The two buildings on the left side of the picture will be demolished next week.

從這裡你可以看見飯店的新地點。圖片的左邊有兩棟建築物，下星期即將要被拆除。

★ 用於描述圖片的詞彙

On the left side of the picture . . .
在圖片左邊

In the upper part of the picture . . .
在圖片的上方

In the middle of the picture . . .
在圖片的中央

C.C. by Art Institute of Chicago

On the right side of the picture . . .
在圖片右邊

In the lower part of the picture . . .
在圖片下方

In the upper left corner of the picture . . .
在圖片的左上方

In the background of the picture . . .
在圖片的背景

In the upper right corner of the picture . . .
在圖片的右上方

In the lower right corner of the picture . . .
在圖片的右下方

In the foreground of the picture . . .
在圖片的前景當中

In the lower left corner of the picture . . .
在圖片的左下方

EXAMPLE 描述照片

This picture shows a family posing for a picture in the backyard. In **the upper left corner of** the picture, you can see the house. The four family members are seated **in the foreground**. The **background** includes a nice-looking lawn and large trees. If you look **on the right side**, it appears that they don't have neighbors. They probably live in a suburb. What a wonderful-looking family!

這是一張在後院拍攝的全家福，在圖片的左上角，你可以看見他們的房子。這一家四口坐在照片的前景中，照片背景有美麗的草坪和大樹。若你看照片的右方，你會發現這家人沒有鄰居，他們可能住在郊區。這家人看起來真是幸福洋溢！

UNIT 13 Explaining Trends
分析事實與數據

講解圖表時，簡報資訊通常包括根據事實與數據（facts and figures）進行趨勢分析。本單元將針對不同的趨勢類型提供常用修辭。

1. Upward and downward 趨升與趨降
2. Fluctuation and stability 波動與穩定
3. Size, speed, and quality 大小、速度與品質
4. Rate of change 變動幅度
5. Approximations 概略值
6. Reasons 根據
7. Bull and bear 多頭市場與空頭市場

---

1 Upward and downward 趨升與趨降

★ 說明趨升與趨降的名詞和動詞：

upward 趨升	
名詞	動詞
① (an) increase 增加	① (to) increase 增加
② (a) rise 上升	② (to) rise 上升
③ (an) improvement 改善	③ (to) reach 升至
④ (an) expansion 擴張	④ (to) go up 上升
⑤ (a) pickup 進步	⑤ (to) shoot up 驟升
⑥ (a) takeoff 起飛	⑥ (to) pick up 進步
⑦ (a) climb 攀升	⑦ (to) grow 成長
	⑧ (to) climb 攀升
	⑨ (to) improve 進步
	⑩ (to) expand 擴張
	⑪ (to) get higher 升高
	⑫ (to) take off（經濟）起飛
	⑬ (to) edge up 向上推進

downward 趨降

名詞	動詞
❶ (a) decrease 減少；衰退	❶ (to) decrease 減少；衰退
❷ (a) reduction 減少	❷ (to) fall 下降
❸ (a) downturn 下降	❸ (to) go down 下跌
❹ (a) fall 下跌	❹ (to) lower 衰減
❺ (a) dive 驟降	❺ (to) lessen 減少
❻ (a) drop 驟跌	❻ (to) shrink 縮減
❼ (a) decline 下降；衰退	❼ (to) cut 削減
❽ (a) plunge 驟跌	❽ (to) plunge 驟跌

★ 說明趨升與趨降還有「名詞片語」和「動詞片語」兩種說法：

Noun Phrase 名詞片語

As this graph shows, there was **an increase/decrease in orders** after March.

Verb Phrase 動詞片語

As this graph shows, **orders increased/decreased** after March.

➤ 據此圖表顯示，三月後的訂單數量增加／減少了。

★ **From . . . to** 的用法

① 「 **from . . . to . . .** 」（從……至……）則是另一個常用於形容時間與數據上升及下降趨勢的句型結構。

① **From** 2020 **to** 2021, there was <u>an increase</u> in expenditures of $10,000.

從 2020 到 2021 年，支出增加了一萬元。 名詞片語

② Total expenditures <u>increased by</u> $10,000 **from** 2020 **to** 2021.

總支出**從** 2020 年**到** 2021 年增加了一萬元。 動詞片語

③ **From** 2008 **to** 2021, there was <u>a drop</u> in foreign investment of about $2 million dollars.

從 2008 年**到** 2021年，外商投資金額減少近兩百萬元。 名詞片語

④ Foreign investment <u>dropped by</u> about $2 million **from** 2008 **to** 2021.

外商投資金額**自** 2008 **至** 2021年間下降近兩百萬元。 動詞片語

② 另一種「 **from . . . to . . .** 」的句型結構，強調重點則是在數據資料。

⑤ This graph shows <u>a slide</u> in revenue **from** $6 **to** $4 million in January.

圖表顯示一月分收益下滑，**從**六百萬減少**至**四百萬。 名詞片語

⑥ Revenue <u>slid **from**</u> $6 **to** $4 million in January, as you can see on the graph.

從圖表上可以看到，一月分的收益**從**六百萬元下滑**至**四百萬元。 動詞片語

③ 使用「 **from . . . to . . .** 」的句型結構來強調數據時，如果需要提及某段時間，可以用「 **during** 」或「 **between** 」之類的單字來加以取代。

⑦ **During** March **and** April, there was <u>a cut</u> in the number of accounts from 45 to 37.

在三月到四月**之間**，客戶數目從 45 減為 37。 名詞片語

⑧ **Between** March **and** April, the number of accounts <u>was cut from</u> 45 <u>to</u> 37.

在三月到四月**間**，客戶數目從 45 減為 37。 動詞片語

④ 最後一種「**from . . . to . . .**」的句型結構，是改變「**from**」和「**to**」的排列順序；此句型只能使用動詞片語：

⑨ Revenue <u>fell</u> 1 percent <u>**from**</u> \$602.9 million a year ago <u>**to**</u> \$596.4 million in the first quarter of this year.

今年第一季總收益下跌1%，**從**一年前的 6 億 290 萬美元降**至** 5 億 9,640 萬美元。　動詞片語

⑩ The stock price <u>rose</u> <u>**to**</u> 73 cents <u>**from**</u> 70 cents a year ago.

股票價格**從**一年前的 70 分升**至** 73 分。　動詞片語

⑤ **名詞片語**後面接介詞「**of**」說明數量，使用**動詞片語**說明則在數字前加「**by**」。

⑪ From 2020 to 2021, there was <u>an increase</u> in expenditures **of** \$10,000.

從 2020 到 2021年，支出**增加**了一萬元。　名詞片語

⑫ Total expenditures <u>increased</u> **by** \$10,000 from 2020 to 2021.

總支出從 2020 年到 2021年**增加**了一萬元。　動詞片語

⑬ From 2014 to 2021, there was <u>a rise</u> in debt **of** almost \$10,000.

從 2014 到 2021年，（公司）**增加**了將近一萬元的負債。　名詞片語

⑭ From 2014 to 2021, debt <u>rose</u> **by** almost \$10,000.

從 2014 到 2021年，負債**增加**將近一萬元。　動詞片語

EXAMPLE (A)

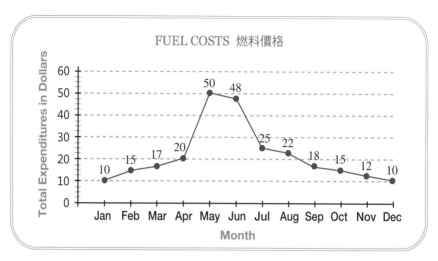

名詞片語 = 動詞片語 =

1 increase (Jan. – Feb.)

N From January to February, there was **an increase** in monthly fuel costs of almost $5.

V From January to February, the monthly fuel cost **increased by** almost $5.

從一月到二月，油價增加了5元。

2 rise (Jan. – Apr.)

N From January to April, there was **a rise** in monthly fuel costs from $10 to $20.

V From January to April, the monthly fuel cost **rose by** $10.

從一月到四月，油價上升了10元。

3 fall (Sep. – Dec.)

N From September to December, there was **a fall** in the monthly fuel cost from $18 to $10.

V From September to December fuel cost **fell by** 8 dollars.

從九月到十二月，油價跌了8元。

4 plunge (May – Jul.)

N From May to July, there was **a plunge** of $25 in the monthly fuel cost.

V From May to July, the monthly fuel cost **plunged** $25.

從五月到七月，油價驟跌了25元。

5 drop off (Jul. – Sep.)

N From July to September, there was **a drop-off** in the monthly fuel cost from $25 to $18.

V From July to September, the monthly fuel cost **dropped off by** $7.

從七月到九月，油價跌了7元。

6 decline (May – Jun.)

N From May to June, there was **a decline** of $2 in the monthly fuel cost.

V From May to June, the monthly fuel cost **declined by** $2.

從五月到六月，油價小跌2元。

EXAMPLE Ⓑ

FUEL COSTS 燃料價格

名詞片語 = Ⓝ　　動詞片語 = Ⓥ

1 during January and February

Ⓝ During January and February, there was **an increase** in the monthly fuel cost from $10 to approximately $15.

Ⓥ Between January and February, the monthly fuel cost **increased** from $10 to approximately $15.

在一到二月間，油價從10元小幅上升至15元。

2 during September and December

N During September and December, there was **a fall** in monthly fuel costs from $18 to $10.

V From September to December, the monthly fuel cost **fell by** $8.

在九月到十二月間油價從18元跌至10元。

3 between June and July

N Between June and July, there was **a plunge** in monthly fuel costs from $48 to $25.

V Between June and July, the monthly fuel cost **plunged** from $48 to $25.

在六到七月間，油價從48元驟跌至25元。

4 between July and September

N Between July and September, there was **a drop-off** in monthly fuel costs from $25 to $18.

V Between July and September, the monthly fuel cost **dropped off** from $25 to $18.

在七月到九月間，油價從25元跌至18元。

5 between May and June

N Between May and June, there was **a decline** in monthly fuel costs from $50 to $48.

V Between May and June, the monthly fuel cost **declined** from $50 to $48.

在五到六月間，油價從50元小幅跌價到48元。

2 Fluctuation and stability 波動與穩定

　　所謂的上升或下降，通常是指在大而複雜的趨勢下，某段時間所呈現的波動或穩定狀態。以下便是常用來形容波動的用語，以及其同義詞彙。

Fluctuation 波動		
peak（最高點）　同義字	• max out • top out	• hit the roof • reach the high point
plunge（驟跌）　同義字	• fall • decline • slide	• decrease • drop
low point（低點）　同義字	• all-time low • lowest level	• rock bottom • nadir
recovery（回復）　同義字	• rebound • turnaround • upturn • revitalization	• recuperation of losses • return to normal • a bounce back • resurgence

　　下圖《學生入學人數表》，包含了上述四種類型的波動。

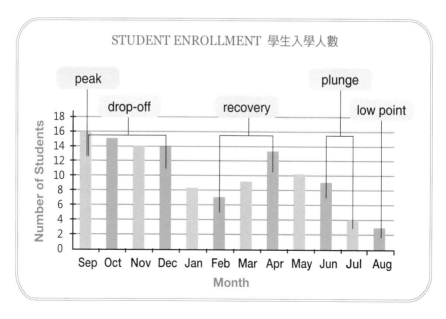

STUDENT ENROLLMENT 學生入學人數

波動在經歷一段時間後便會回復到穩定狀態。以下是經常用來形容「**情況回穩**」的用語。

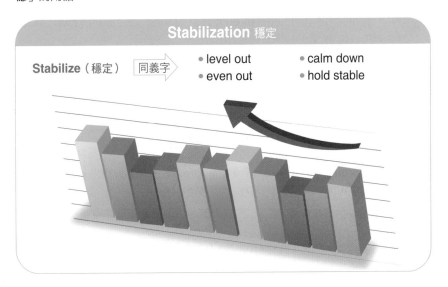

如下圖所示，我們預期從四月開始收益將逐漸成長，後半年業績持續呈現穩定狀態。我們也預估從七月起獲利會開始趨於穩定，從約25,000元成長到約27,000元。

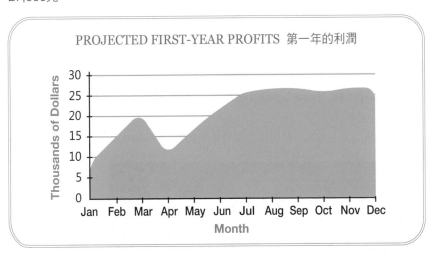

要説明**長期呈現穩定的趨勢**，可以使用 remain steady 和 remain constant（持續維持穩定）等用語。

① Stabilize 穩定

① By July, monthly profits will **even out** at around $25,000 and will **remain steady** thereafter.

到了七月分，收益會**趨穩**達 25,000 元，之後持續呈現**穩定**狀態。

② Monthly profits **leveled out** at a higher rate in July and then **remained constant** until the end of the year.

七月時利潤會**穩定**在高點，一直到年底都**持續穩定**狀態。

③ Monthly profits should **stabilize** at approximately $25,000 in July and should **continue to be steady** afterward.

七月開始收益應該會**穩定**達到 25,000 元，其後將**繼續維持平穩**。

④ As long as the demand **continues (remains constant)**, we'll be successful.

只要有**穩定**的需求量，我們就能成功。

② Recovery 回穩

⑤ The market should **bounce back (rebound)** in September.

市場在九月應該會**回溫**。

⑥ We expect a strong **upturn (turnaround)** in sales when the new product line comes out.

當新產品線上市時，我們預期業績會明顯地**回升**。

③ Peak 最高點

⑦ We sold the stock when it **peaked (reached its highest point)**.

我們在股市**高點**賣了股票。

④ Low point 最低點

⑧ When the stock **bottomed out (reached its lowest point)** below 20 points, we were surprised.

當股價**跌破**千分之二時，我們都很驚訝。

⑨ Our losses **reached an all-time low (rock bottom)** in September.

我們的虧損在九月達到**新低**。

⑩ Production speed **topped out (maxed out)** at 57 units per month.

每月**最大**的生產量是 57 單位。

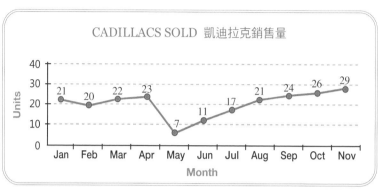

CADILLACS SOLD 凱迪拉克銷售量

	月間發展趨勢	
January to mid-April	Business as usual
Mid-April to mid-May	Competitor has a going-out-of-business sale that he calls the *I Must Be Out of My Mind With Prices This Low* sale
Mid-May to mid-November	Recovery from the competition's sale; increased popularity of low-mileage, politically incorrect cars

Between January and mid-April, it was business as usual, with very little fluctuation. During the next month however, our competitor had a going-out-of-business sale that he called the I Must Be Out of My Mind With Prices This Low sale. Our sales plummeted from 23 cars in April to only 7 in May. After that, we recovered steadily. Sales rose at an impressive rate because of the increased popularity of low-mileage, politically incorrect cars. From May to November, monthly sales rose from 7 cars to 29 cars.

在一月至四月中期間，業績一切正常，波動不大。但在接下來的五月，我們的競爭對手進行結束營業特賣會，打出「瘋狂低價特賣」的口號，我們的生意因此受到影響，從四月分的23輛車，滑落到五月分的7輛。五月過後，我們從對手結束拍賣的衝擊中回穩。銷售量直線上升，其主因與低里程的豪華新車款逐漸受到消費者歡迎有關。從五月至十一月，銷售車量從7輛升至29輛。

3 Size, speed, and quality 大小、速度與品質

無論是呈現上升或下降、穩定或浮動，趨勢的變更都必須從波動的大小、速度和品質等方面說明，而這些用於說明的詞彙通常是形容詞或副詞。

adjective 形容詞	**Size 大小**	adverb 副詞
最大 ↓ 最小 • enormous • substantial • considerable • modest • significant • slight • infinitesimal		最大 ↓ 最小 • enormously • substantially • considerably • modestly • significantly • slightly • infinitesimally

例句

- a <u>substantial</u> plunge in profit
- a <u>slight</u> decline in profit
- an <u>enormous</u> rise in profit
- a <u>considerable</u> increase in profit

例句

- Profits plunged <u>substantially</u>.
- Profits declined <u>slightly</u>.
- Profits rose <u>enormously</u>.
- Profits increased <u>considerably</u>.

adjective 形容詞	**Speed 速度**	adverb 副詞
最快 ↓ 最慢 • rapid • swift • steady • gradual • sluggish		最快 ↓ 最慢 • rapidly • swiftly • steadily • gradually • sluggishly

例句

- a <u>swift</u> plunge in profit
- a <u>gradual</u> decline in profit
- a <u>rapid</u> rise in profit
- a <u>steady</u> increase in profit

例句

- Profits plunged <u>swiftly</u>.
- Profits declined <u>gradually</u>.
- Profits rose <u>sluggishly</u>.
- Profits increased <u>steadily</u>.

adjective 形容詞	Quality 品質	adverb 副詞
最好 ↓ 最差 • spectacular • exceptional • great • encouraging • marginal • disappointing • catastrophic		最好 ↓ 最差 • spectacularly • exceptionally • greatly • encouragingly • marginally • disappointingly • catastrophically

例句

- a <u>catastrophic</u> plunge in profit
- a <u>disappointing</u> decline in profit
- a <u>spectacular</u> rise in profit
- a <u>great</u> increase in profit

例句

- Profits plunged <u>catastrophically</u>.
- Profits <u>disappointingly</u> declined.
- Profits rose <u>spectacularly</u>.
- Profits increased <u>greatly</u>.

① In this diagram, you can see a **substantial** rise in consumer spending after the free trade agreement.

在這個圖表中，各位可以看出在簽訂自由貿易協議後，消費者支出呈現**大幅**成長。

② In this diagram, you can see that consumer spending rose **substantially** after the free trade agreement.

現在請看這個圖表，各位可以看出在簽訂自由貿易協議後，消費者支出**大幅地**成長。

123

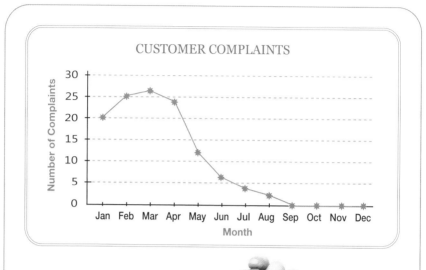

CUSTOMER COMPLAINTS

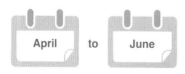

① During the months of January to March, complaints about service rose significantly, from 20 to 26.

一月到三月間，客訴服務不周的件數顯著上升，從20件上升到26件。

....

② In April, the number of complaints started to decrease. Then in May and June, they dropped off substantially, from 24 to just 6.

四月分時，客訴件數開始減少。到了五、六月時，已經大幅下降，從原本的24件降低到6件。

③ Between July and September, there was a gradual decline in the number of complaints, from 4 to 0.

在七月到九月期間，客訴件數漸漸下滑，從4件降到零。

④ From October to December, the number of complaints stabilized at 0.

十月到十二月一直都維持在零客訴的狀態。

4 Rate of change 變動幅度

談到趨勢的波動，通常也會討論到變動的比率，你可以說明**成長率**（growth rate），或是說明**下降率**（rate of decline）。

① For chip manufacturers, 2019 was a rebound year with an **overall growth rate of** 19.5 percent.

對晶片製造商而言，2019 是起死回生的一年，**總成長率達** 19.5%。

② Revenues **declined by** 6.8 percent last quarter.

上一季的收益**下滑** 6.8%。

③ U.S. nonfinancial debt **grew at** an annual rate of 7.3 percent in the first quarter.

美國第一季年度非金融負債比率**增長**了 7.3%。

④ Looking at the **rate of decline** in child poverty between 2020 and 2021, the sharpest drop occurred for children in female-householder families.

觀察 2020 至 2021 年間兒童貧困的**下降率**，下降比率最劇烈的部分都出現在由女性擔任一家之主的家庭。

⑤ The amount of ice formed in the Arctic winter **has declined sharply** in the last two years.

北極地區冬季結冰的數量在過去兩年間**大幅縮減**。

另一種特殊的成長率類型是**複合年平均增長率**（Compound Annual Growth Rate），是說明一項投資在某段時間內的年度增長率，通常直接簡稱為 **CAGR**。

⑥ According to the report, the global market for AI in education is likely to grow at a **CAGR** of 47% over the next five years.

報告顯示，在接下來的五年中，人工智慧應用在教育的國際市場將以 47% 的**複合年平均增長率**增加。

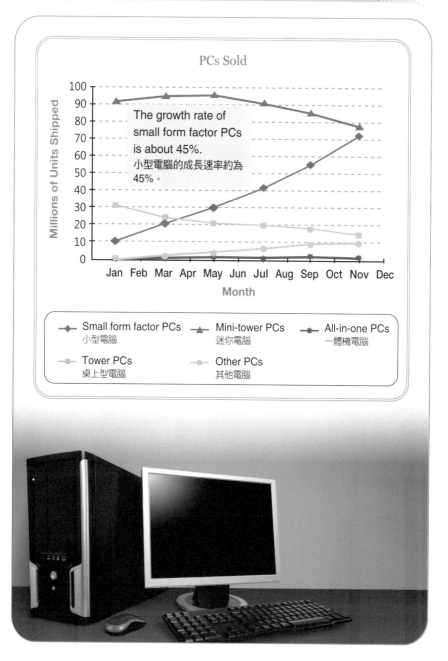

PCs Sold

The growth rate of
small form factor PCs
is about 45%.
小型電腦的成長速率約為
45%。

Millions of Units Shipped

Month

Small form factor PCs
小型電腦

Mini-tower PCs
迷你電腦

All-in-one PCs
一體機電腦

Tower PCs
桌上型電腦

Other PCs
其他電腦

第一句

➤ a description that introduces the subject or main idea of the graph

描述此折線圖的主要論點或主題

① This graph illustrates the swiftly rising growth rate of small form factor PCs compared with the growth rates of other PC types.

本圖顯示出小型電腦與其他電腦比較之下，出貨數量在短時間內上升較快。

第二、三句

➤ for **identification** of and **commentary** on the small form factor growth rate, with specific references to the growth rate and number of units shipped

證明與評論小型電腦的體型與運貨量多寡的關聯

② As you can see, the small form factor growth rate is about 45%, increasing from 10 million units shipped in January to more than 70 million units shipped in November.

小型電腦的出貨成長率為45%，從一月的一千萬台成長到十一月的七千萬台。

③ This growth rate is significantly better than that of other PC types, so we should focus more effort on the small form factor PC segment.

這樣的成長率顯著優於其他種類的電腦，我們應該致力於開發小型電腦。

第四、五句

➤ a description of another PC type—one sentence to **identify** the type and another for **commenting**

描寫一種其他種類電腦的出貨量；一句描繪此種類，另一句評論

④ Look now at tower PCs. That rate is declining gradually!

請看桌上型主機電腦的折線圖，其出貨量是逐漸下降的！

⑤ So that's another reason to concentrate more on small form factor PCs.

這也是我們該致力開發小型電腦的另一原因。

5 Approximations 概略值

在説明圖表所呈現的趨勢變動時，通常會以較廣泛的概念説明數據資料。太過詳細的數字是不必要的，且對大多數人而言，**概括的數值反而更容易記憶**，例如，把 35.2 説成「大約三分之一」；998,543 則可説成「將近一百萬」。

數據／概略值表			
Figure 數據	Approximation 概略值	Figure 數據	Approximation 概略值
66%	about two-thirds of 約三分之二	1,043	more than a thousand 一千多
28%	just over a quarter of 四分之一多	115	more than a hundred 一百多
56%	just over half of 一半多	19	fewer than twenty 將近 20
49%	just under half of 幾乎一半	2	a couple 幾個
74%	almost three-quarters of 接近四分之三	3	a few 一點
33.3333%	a third of 三分之一	6	several 一些
92%	most of 絕大多數	749,982	about three-quarters of a million 將近 75 萬
98.5%	almost all 將近全部	1,256,890,534	more than 1.2 billion 超過 12 億

★ 數據資料慣用規則

① **當分母大於 5 時，不要用分數說明。**

多數人都知道 1/2 就是 50%，3/4 是 75%，但是很少有人會想到 1/6 約等於 16%，或 7/8 等於 87.5%。

② 分數的**分子大於 2** 時，別忘了在**字尾加上 s**。

two-thirds of the students	三分之二的學生
three-quarters of the proceeds	四分之三的收益

③ 大多的分數都和介系詞 **of** 連用。

three-quarters **of** the employees	四分之三的員工

④ **many** 用於可數名詞，**much** 用於不可數名詞。

We have too **many** chairs.	我們有太多椅子了。
We have too **much** information.	我們有過多的資訊。

⑤ **fewer** 用於可數名詞，**less** 用於不可數名詞。

We used to have **fewer** chairs.	我們之前的椅子比較少。
We used to have **less** information.	我們過去獲得的訊息較少。

⑥ 分數前的冠詞通常用 **a**，不用 one。

a third of the citizens	三分之一的市民

⑦ half 前面，**則不加 a 或 one**。

Half of the funds were bought.	一半的基金都已經被買下了。

6 Reasons 根據

簡報時，能**提出特定根據**是十分重要的。

★ 隱含**因果關係**的片語有以下幾種，**後面接名詞片語**以說明**原因**：

- is a result of 是……造成的結果
- due to 由於
- is caused by 由……造成

① This increase in sales volume **is the result of** a discount in the retail price.

總業績的成長是零售價格打折促銷後的**結果**。

② The plummeting stock price **is due to** political instability.

股價崩跌**源於**政局不穩。

③ Our financial success **was caused by** a change in the tax law.

我們在財務上的成功要**歸因於**稅法的修改。

★ 其他類似修辭片語用法和前述修辭相反，**後面接趨勢變化的結果**：

- lead to 導致
- give rise to 促成
- is the reason for 是造成……的原因

④ A discount in the retail price **led to** an increase in sales volume.

零售價格的折扣**帶來**總業績的成長。

⑤ Political instability **gave rise to** the plummeting stock price.

政局的不穩定**導致**股價突然下跌。

⑥ The change in the tax law **is the reason** for our financial success.

稅法的修改**是**財務成功**的主因**。

★ 另一種簡單能**表明原由**的修辭，使用連接詞「**and**」和「**because**」連接句子。

⑦ We discounted retail prices, **and** sales volume increased.

零售價打折後，我們的總業績**便**成長了。

⑧ The stock price plummeted **because** the political climate became unstable.

股價下跌是**因為**政局不穩定。

⑨ The tax law changed, **and** our finances improved.

稅法經過修改，**而**財經也獲得成功的改善。

PROFITS FOR FIGURINE BUSINESS
陶瓷公仔的利潤

Assumption 假定	• The company is an importer of ceramic figurines. • The company's monthly profits increased, decreased, or stabilized because of the reasons listed below. • The unit on the graph is thousands of dollars.
Reasons 利潤波動原因	• **First quarter:** Initial popularity of the product • **Second quarter:** New competitors entering the market; supply problems • **Third quarter:** Fly-by-night competitors dropping out of the market; finding better suppliers • **Fourth quarter:** Continual opening up of new markets

1st Qtr 第一季

Monthly profits rose rapidly from approximately $10,000 to more than $20,000 during the first quarter because of the initial popularity of the ceramic figurines.

第一季的月銷售量從1萬元升至2萬多，因為陶瓷公仔在初期很受大眾歡迎。

 2nd Qtr 第二季

After March, profits started to drop off significantly as a result of new competitors entering the market and supply problems.

三月分之後，因為競爭對手此時進入市場，供應商方面也出了問題，利潤開始大幅降低。

 3rd Qtr 第三季

Profits declined to rock bottom at the end of May and then bounced back, building up from less than $10,000 in June to more than $25,000 in September. This huge turnaround can be attributed to the fly-by-night competitors dropping out of the market and our use of better suppliers.

到了五月底利潤驟降至最低點，但之後開始回升，從六月分低於1萬元升到九月分的2萬5千元。利潤的大幅回升是源自於投機競爭者退出市場，以及找到更好的供應商。

 4th Qtr 第四季

In the fourth quarter, the continual opening of new markets brought about a period of stability, with monthly profits leveling off at more than $25,000 and remaining constant for the last three months of the year.

在第四季時，許多新的市場陸續被開發，使得這三個月內利潤一直保持在2萬5千多元。

7 Bull and bear 多頭市場與空頭市場

財經的走勢常用「**bull market**」（多頭市場）與「**bear market**」（空頭市場）說明。

Bull Market 指投資人對市場懷抱**充分信心**，相信購買的股票價格及資產都會增加。若是市場的氣氛是 **bullish**（**樂觀的、看漲的**），則大部分投資人都會預期股市上漲。

① **A bullish** surge for IBM may occur because of recent e-Business trends.

由於近期企業電子化的趨勢， 人們預期 IBM 股價將**會飆漲**。

② After the software developers' conference, **I am very bullish** about Apple.

在參加軟體研發人員會議後，**我對**蘋果電腦的股票行情**非常有信心**。

③ America's **raging bull market** continued its astonishing run today.

美國**走勢大好的股市**今日持續飆漲。

「**bear market**」（空頭市場）的意義和前者正好相反，投資人對股市未來發展持**悲觀態度**。為了減少損失，投資人拋售股票，市場趨勢朝負面發展，產生通貨膨脹、對未來通貨膨脹持預期心理、衝動性消費、借貸型消費、存款不足與負債增加等情況。

④ Gold has been **in a major bear market** since May of this year.

今年五月開始，黃金在**市場的走勢大跌**。

⑤ The rate went up nearly 1%, **ending the bear market**.

股價上升近 1%，**結束長期下跌的趨勢**。

⑥ **The bear market** has scared investors away.

委靡不振的股市前景，嚇跑了投資人。

在股市一片漲勢下，暫時的跌停稱作「**correction**」（回落），對於 correction 的定義通常是指**跌幅高於 10%**，但低於 **20%**。

⑦ We will likely see a **correction** in 2014 before the bull market resumes.

在股市回漲之前，極有可能於 2014 年**暫時下跌**。

⑧ This dip in the bull market trend represents the **correction**.

在股價高漲的趨勢下，這次的下跌屬於**短期的回落**。

⑨ The bull market **corrected** itself during the fourth quarter.

持續上漲的股市於第四季**暫時回落**。

⋯⋯

而當股市持續跌停時（空頭市場），股票短期上漲則稱為「**bear market rally**」（股市重振）。

⑩ The **bear market rally** will lead many to believe it is safe to buy back in again.

股價重振會讓投資者相信重回股市交易是安全的。

History shows that the market typically moves in cycles. In the last century, there have been three bull markets (shown in grey) and three bear markets.

從歷史紀錄看來，股市走勢通常是循環性的。在上一世紀，出現了三次多頭市場（以灰色表示），以及三次空頭市場。

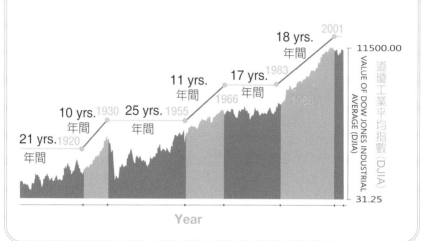

① The 1920s were extremely **bullish**.

1920 年代的股市走勢大好。

② The period from 1966 to 1983 has been characterized as **a prolonged bear market**.

1966 年到 1983 年間，股市走勢持續不振。

③ The 18-year bull market that occurred between 1983 and 2001 had several notable **corrections** including a substantial decline after 1986.

1983 年到 2001 年這 18 年間股市有數次較大的回落，包括 1986 年後的重挫。

④ A strong **bear market rally** rang in the beginning of the 18-year bull market that occurred between 1983 and 2001.

一次的股市重振開啟 1983 年到 2001 年長達 18 年的多頭市場。

UNIT 14 Definition and Restatement
簡述簡報相關定義並重申要點

在高科技簡報中若出現艱深的資訊、術語（jargon）、語意不明的縮寫（acronym），
或是任何觀眾也許不甚了解的主題，都需要講者進一步地解釋其重要性。

★ 你可以**直接向觀眾解說**他們**不熟悉的字詞**。

① The excavation finally revealed the mastaba, **which is** an oblong structure with a flat roof built over a mummy chamber or burial pit.

考古挖掘最終揭露了古埃及密室的真面目，**也就是**搭建於木乃伊墓室或墓地上方，一座屋頂平坦的矩形建物。

★ 你更可以在需要解說的字後面，直接**加上其解釋**。

② The excavation finally revealed the mastaba, an oblong structure with a flat roof built over a mummy chamber or burial pit.

考古挖掘最終揭露了古埃及密室的真面目——那是搭建於木乃伊墓室或墓地上方，一座屋頂平坦的矩形建物。

★ 你也可以用下列的方法**解釋字義**：

③ The excavation finally revealed **an oblong structure with a flat roof, known as** a mastaba, over the mummy chamber or burial pit.

考古挖掘最終揭露了一座屋頂平坦的矩形建物，**稱之為**古埃及密室，就建於木乃伊墓室或墓地上方。

★ 有些字雖然**不屬於專業領域**，但也許對聽眾來說很陌生，你可以**用更常見好懂的方式**直接重述它。

④ The king's laws were often **arbitrary; in other words**, he made rules on the basis of how he felt at the moment.

國王制定的法律通常是專制武斷的；**換句話說**，他是依照自己當時的看法來訂定。

⑤ The **jarheads, that is**, the marines, were killed by a roadside bomb.

一些鍋蓋頭，**也就是**美國海軍陸戰隊，被路邊的炸彈炸死。

⑥ WASP **is an acronym for** white Anglo Saxon Protestant. The term has
largely negative connotations.

WASP是盎格魯‧撒克遜系白人新教徒（white Anglo Saxon Protestant）
的縮寫。這個字大致帶有負面含義。

⑦ Wiskott-Aldrich syndrome protein, **or** WASP, is a 502 - amino acid
protein expressed in the cells of the hematopoietic system.

威斯科特－奧爾德里奇二氏綜合症蛋白（Wiskott-Aldrich syndrome protein），
或稱 WASP，是產生於造血系統細胞內，502 序列的氨基酸蛋白。

⑧ Women Airforce Service Pilots, **also known as** WASPs, were a
pioneering organization of female paramilitary pilots.

女子航空勤務飛行隊（Women Airforce Service Pilots），**也稱為** WASP，
是史上最早的民間女性軍機飛行隊。

⑨ W.A.S.P. **stands for** We Are Satan's People, the name of an American heavy metal band from the 1980s.

W.A.S.P. **代表**「我們是撒旦信奉者（We Are Satan's People）」，是美國 1980 年代一個重金屬樂團的名稱。

⑩ According to lead singer Blackie Lawless, W.A.S.P. **refers to the phrase** "We ain't sure, pal."

根據主唱 Blackie Lawless 所説，W.A.S.P. **指的是**「我們不確定，朋友 （We ain't sure, pal.）」這個詞語。

★ **縮寫的讀法**各有不同。

- 把每個英文字分開來唸：USA、CIA、KGB
- 把部分英文簡寫分開唸，部分合成一個單字唸：JPEG、MPEG、ASAP
- 把所有英文當作一個單字發音：AIDS、ECFA、SARS

要搞清楚每個縮寫字的讀法，要是沒有唸對正確的發音，會混淆觀眾視聽，也會讓他們會懷疑你的專業度。

UNIT 15 Giving Examples
提供範例

簡報常需要範例以解釋主題。範例可讓難懂晦澀的術語變得具有意義，讓聽眾更輕易地了解簡報主旨。

以下是舉例時**常用的英文詞彙和其例句**：

★ **such as**

① Our science class is studying crustaceans, **such as** shrimps, crabs, and lobsters.

我們的自然課正在研究甲殼綱動物，**例如**蝦子、螃蟹與龍蝦。

② Products made from paper **such as** a lunch box and a newspaper can be recycled.

紙類產品**例如**午餐盒和報紙都可以回收。

★ **like**

③ Precious stones, **like** rubies and diamonds, cannot be cut with a knife or scratched with glass.

寶石，**像**紅寶石和鑽石，是不能用刀子切割或是被玻璃刮傷的。

④ Some entertainers, **like** Madonna and Lady Gaga, are famous all over the world.

有些藝人，**像**瑪丹娜和女神卡卡，風靡全球。

★ include

⑤ Treatment of CIA detainees in secret EU prisons **included** solitary confinement, constant shackling, poor-quality food, and lack of clothing.

中情局囚犯在歐聯的秘密監獄中所遭受的對待**包括**單獨監禁、經常性綁上手鐐腳銬、粗劣的伙食與被迫裸身長達數週。

⑥ Smartphones now **include** technologies that were once sold only as separate devices, including cameras and MP3 players.

現今智慧型手機將過去分別販售的產品功能做了統合，**包括**相機和MP3播放器的功能。

★ for instance

⑦ Threatened coral—**for instance**, staghorn and elkhorn species—were once very prominent.

瀕臨絕跡的珊瑚，**例如**鹿角珊瑚和麋角珊瑚，在過去曾經大量繁衍。

⑧ Countries in the Middle East, Iraq and Iran **for instance**, are rich in oil.

中東國家，**例如**伊拉克和伊朗，富產石油。

★ for example

⑨ They excelled at sports requiring endurance: **for example**, long-distance swimming and running.

他們在需要耐力的運動項目上取得卓越成績，**例如**長泳和賽跑。

⑩ Freeway traffic is at its worst on important holidays, **for example**, Chinese New Year and Tomb Sweeping Day.

高速公路車況在重要假期時最糟，**例如**在農曆新年和清明節時。

UNIT 16 Emphasizing Significant Points
強調重要論點

簡報中某些論點比起其他要點更為重要，需要特別強調才能突顯其意義。
用來強調「加強重點」的用語如下：

1. Direct language 直接用語
2. Adverb-verb phrases 副詞——動詞片語
3. Adverb-adjective phrases 副詞——形容詞片語
4. Intensification 加強語氣
5. De-contraction and auxiliaries 去縮約型式與助動詞
6. Spotlight 聚焦

1 Direct language 直接用語

要強調論點最直截了當的方式，就是使用**直接用語**（direct language）。

★ **significant/significance** 重要的／重要性

① I want to emphasize how **significant** this point is.
我想要強調這個論點的**重要性**。

② I can't stress the **significance** of this point enough.
這個論點十分**重要**，需要再三強調。

③ I'd like to call your attention to the **significance** of this point.
我想讓各位注意到這個論點的**重要性**。

★ **important** 重要的

④ Let me emphasize how **important** this point will be in the future.
讓我來強調這個論點在未來的**重要性**。

★ **insignificant** 不重要的

⑤ I'd like to emphasize to you that this point is totally **insignificant**.

我想要跟你強調的是，這個論點完全**不重要**。

★ 更多**可在直接用語中使用的形容詞**

Significant 重要的

同義字
- important
- vital
- serious
- prominent
- critical
- meaningful
- crucial
- remarkable
- noteworthy

反義字
- insignificant
- inconsequential
- immaterial
- meaningless
- pointless
- minor
- trivial
- unimportant
- trifling

2 Adverb-verb phrases 副詞──動詞片語

副詞可以**強化一篇論述**，加倍**強調論點**。

★ 檢視下面兩個句子的**不同處**：

原句
> I **suggest** you **reorganize** middle management.
> 我**建議**你**重新整合**中階管理部門。

原句加上副詞
──動詞片語
> I **strongly suggest** you **totally reorganize** middle management.
> 我**強烈建議**你**徹底重新整合**中階管理部門。

★ 在某些情況下，**副詞可以加在動詞之後**：

① The market price is **dropping steadily,** and it probably won't recover.

市價**逐漸在下跌**，而且未來很可能無法恢復。

② The bad weather **began immediately** after I arrived.

天氣在我抵達之後，**開始迅速**轉壞。

★ 副詞和動詞固定搭配使用：

③ I **deeply regret** having to end the contract prematurely.

我**深感後悔**提早結束合約。

④ He **honestly believes** that we will recover our losses next year.

他**由衷相信**明年我們的虧損將能被彌補。

⑤ The bank **utterly refused** the application.

銀行**完全拒絕**我們的申請。

更多副詞—動詞片語

- completely agree 完全同意
- fall dramatically 急遽下跌
- fully realize 完全了解
- firmly oppose to 堅決反對
- sincerely hope 衷心希望
- freely admit 大方承認

- rise sharply 急遽上升
- enthusiastically endorse 熱情支持
- totally reject 全盤拒絕
- level off immediately 立即平穩
- sincerely believe 衷心相信

3 Adverb-adjective phrases 副詞—形容詞片語　（36）

用副詞**修飾形容詞片語**能夠更強化字義。

★ 請比較下列兩個句子：

| 原句 | ▶ | I want to emphasize the **significant** nature of this point.
我想要強調此論點本身的**重要性**。 |

| 原句加上「**副詞
—形容詞片語**」 | ▶ | I want to emphasize the **highly significant** nature of this point.
我想要強調此論點本身的**極度重要性**。 |

① You must realize that these figures are **extremely important**.

你必須了解這些數字**非常重要**。

② Let me emphasize how **utterly essential** the sale is to this year's profit margin.

我要強調銷售額對今年利潤率的**絕對重要性**。

③ The terms of the deal are **totally unacceptable** to our friends in Kazakhstan.

這筆交易的條件對哈薩克的合作夥伴是**完全無法接受的**。

更多副詞—形容詞片語

- utterly appalling 十分恐怖的
- totally revolutionary 完全創新的
- extremely broad 極度廣泛的
- exceedingly bullish 極度樂觀的
- absolutely unbearable
  完全無法接受的

4 Intensification 加強語氣

　　在英文中，「**增強用語**」本身沒有什麼意義，但卻可以增強其修飾字義的語氣，通常會**置於其修飾單字之前**，最常見的英文增強用語是「**very**」。

① It's **quite** hot today in Nigeria.

奈及利亞今天**相當**炎熱。

② The contractor is **so** busy right now.

承包商現在**非常**忙碌。

③ This latest suggestion is **just** perfect!

這個最新的建議**實在**太棒了！

④ The manager has never seen **such** highly motivated workers.

該主管從未見過**如此**上進的勞工。

⑤ I'm a **little** frustrated with her constant complaining.

我對她接二連三的抱怨**有一點**不悅。

⑥ Recently, business has been **a bit** slow.

最近我們的生意**有些**不振。

⑦ That report was **pretty** good!

那篇報導**挺**不錯的！

⑧ The factory just got **brand** new equipment.

那間工廠才剛引進**全**新器材。

⑨ This price isn't **even** close to the real value.

這個價格**甚至**不及實際價值。

⑩ If the **entire** network goes down, we're in **big** trouble.

若**整個**網路損毀，我們就麻煩**大**了。

⑪ With **constant** virus protection, your computer is **pretty** secured.

只要**持續**有防毒軟體的防護，你的電腦就**滿**安全的。

⑫ A **dramatic** rise in orders precipitated our need for a **totally** automated system.

大幅增加的訂單讓我們急需**全**自動的系統。

⑬ These figures are **highly** significant, and maintaining this performance level is **absolutely** crucial to future success.

這些數據**非常**重要，而維持類似的營運狀況對於未來的成功**非常**重要。

⑭ The board **completely** agrees that a **full** recovery is **very** unlikely.

董事會**完全**同意要**全面**恢復是**不太**可能的。

⑮ The **whole** project has failed **badly**, but the situation could get **even** worse.

整個計劃案**徹底**失敗，但情況可能還會**更**糟。

⑯ The **actual** chance of **noticeable** improvement is **extremely** slim.

要能**明顯**改善的**實際**機率**非常**微薄。

....

強化用語 **at all**（根本）和 **whatsoever**（一點都不；毫不……），會接在要修飾的形容詞**之後**。

⑰ His speech on cross-strait relations is not important **whatsoever**.

他在演講中所談論的兩岸關係議題**絲毫**不重要。

⑱ It's not viable **at all** to continue giving financial aid to countries that are abusing the situation.

對於濫用現況的國家，給予經濟援助**根本**是不可行的。

5 De-contraction and auxiliaries 去縮約型式與助動詞

　　你可以替動詞加**重音**，來強調平日會話時發音會簡略帶過的**縮約字**（contraction）。以下列句子為例，你可以將「it's」去縮約型式後，把重音強調在「is」這個動詞上。

① It's important to diversify our investments.
> It **is** important to diversify our investments.

將我們公司的資金投資在不同市場是很重要的。

....

　　把 **am**、**is**、**are**、**was**、**were**、**has**、**have** 這類動詞加上重音時，都帶有**強調**的意味。

② I'm confident that a solution exists.
> I **am** confident that a solution exists.

我深信一定有解決的方法。

③ There's a possibility of failure.
> There **is** a possibility of failure.

的確有失敗的可能性。

④ We've been through this situation before.
> We **have** been through this situation before.

我們之前也遇過這種情況。

⑤ We're still in the process of collecting the fees.
> We **are** still in the process of collecting the fees.

我們仍然在收帳的程序中。

....

　　在帶有**否定意義**的句子中，會去除縮約字的型式，並將重音加強在**表否定的去縮約字**上，例如 **not** 這個字。

⑥ The consultation wasn't productive.
> The consultation was **not** productive.

這次的諮商並沒有達到效果。

⑦ It isn't the right direction for the company.
➤ It is **not** the right direction for the company.

這不是公司應該走的方向。

⑧ We didn't sell the stock soon enough.
➤ We did **not** sell the stock soon enough.

我們拋售股票的動作不夠迅速。

⑨ The board mustn't approve the deal.
➤ The board must **not** approve the deal.

董事會絕對不會同意這筆交易。

⑩ Next year, we won't be able to purchase the same amount.
➤ Next year, we will **not** be able to purchase the same amount.

我們明年不會再採購同樣的數量。

★ 助動詞也可以置於句中來**加強語氣**，助動詞後要加原形動詞。

⑪ The shipment arrived last month.
➤ The shipment **did** arrive last month.

貨運已於上個月抵達。

⑫ The speech begins at 3:00 p.m.
➤ The speech **will** begin at 3:00 p.m.

演講將於下午三點進行。

⑬ They'd prefer to get our input ASAP.
➤ They **would** prefer to get our input ASAP.

他們希望能盡快得到我們的意見回覆。

6 Spotlight 聚焦

「**what . . . is . . .**」的句型也很適合用來**加強語氣**。此句型會引導聽眾注意重點是那些，用「聚焦」的方式來集中加強語氣。

① We don't want to rush this decision.
  ➤ **What** we don't want to do **is** rush this decision.

  我們不必急著做出決定。

② We have to consider the long-term goals.
  ➤ **What** we have to do **is** consider the long-term goals.

  我們必須要做的是考慮我們的長期目標。

上述句子中，說話者（speaker）強調主事者（agent）需加強句子中的動作。但一個沒有主事者的句子，也可以用「**what . . . is . . .**」的句型結構來**強調**。

③ It's important to always be closing sales.
  ➤ **What** is important **is** to always be closing sales.

  不斷成交買賣是十分重要的。

④ It matters a lot if the target is missed, even by a small amount.
  ➤ **What** matters a lot **is** if the target is missed, even by a small amount.

  即使只差一點就達成目標，仍會造成很大的影響。

154

通常使用「**what . . . is . . .**」句型結構的句子與出現在它之前的句子，有著**完全相反（相對）**的句義。

⑤ They can take the tablet market. **What** we won't let them do **is** compete with us for notebooks.

他們可以搶得平板電腦市場，但我們必須阻止他們和我們競爭筆記型電腦市場。

⑥ Faster shipping might have helped yesterday. **What** will help today **is** an accurate inventory.

在此之前，改善配送速度也許會有幫助；現在我們需要的是正確的產品庫存清單。

⑦ We can't sustain these losses much longer. **What** we can do **is** cut our losses and reinvest our remaining capital.

我們無法再繼續承受這些損失，我們現在能做的是減少虧損並重新投資剩餘資本。

⑧ Last year's results are insignificant. **What** matters now **is** the future.

去年的結果並不重要，現在該注重的是未來。

⑨ I'll go to the next conference. **What** I won't do **is** purchase the amount of raw material that they require.

我會去下一場會議，但我不會答應購買他們要求的原料數量。

⑩ You've brought donuts. **What** you haven't brought **is** coffee!

你已經帶了甜甜圈，可是還欠咖啡！

UNIT 17 Contextualizing a Point
整合重點

你可以在某段前後文中呈現出一個具體的概念，像是時間、金錢、人員、勞動市場、政府策略或是其他項目，並且從中傳達一個定義明確的訊息。

1. Direct language 直接用語
2. Sentence adverbs 修飾整句的副詞
3. Sentence qualifier phrases 修飾片語

1 Direct language 直接用語

在特定段落**加入重點**時，可以採用**直接用語**（direct language）來告訴聽眾你接下來的做法，詳加說明你將**如何**解釋你的重點。

① Let me put this in a **technical context.** Recycling is . . .

就**技術性層面**而言，回收是……

② I'll explain this in **economic terms**. Recycling is . . .

以**經濟面向**來解釋，回收是……

③ **The political ramifications** shouldn't be overlooked. Recycling is . . .

政治後果是不可被忽視的，回收是……

④ I'll put this in **financial terms**.

讓我用**財經的方式**解釋。

以上的例句以**形容詞**來修飾前後文的完整語句。接下來介紹的句子將有一些改變，使用**直接用語**來形容相關職業，或是其他能定義前後文的角色。

⑤ From an **engineer's** point of view, recycling is . . .

就**工程師**的立場來說，回收是……

⑥ From a **teacher's** perspective, recycling is . . .

就**教師**的觀點來看，回收是……

⑦ If you consider the **customer**, recycling is . . .

如果考慮到**顧客**的立場，回收是……

⑧ For the **average person**, recycling is . . .

對於**一般人**來說，回收是……

⑨ To a **doctor**, the method is unsafe.

對於**醫生**而言，這種方法是不安全的。

2 Sentence adverbs 修飾整句的副詞

　　修飾整句的副詞（sentence adverbs）是置於句首的副詞，作用在**連接**其後的句子。這種修飾型副詞能讓聽眾即刻了解你的看法，譬如要採用某種特殊觀點來呈現主題時，可以使用「(**sentence adverb**) + **speaking . . .**」的句型。

① **Environmentally speaking**, traveling frequently by air is one of the worst things you can do.

　　就環保而言，頻繁的飛航旅行是很糟糕的事情。

② **Morally speaking**, holding enemy combatants without charges and torturing them has ruined their reputation abroad.

　　就道德上來說，拘留無罪的敵軍並加以折磨，已經損害了他們在海外的名聲。

③ **Geographically speaking**, Canada is the second-largest country on Earth.

　　從地理學來說，加拿大是全世界第二大的國家。

更多不同主題背景的副詞修飾語

- Biologically 生物學地
- Commercially 商業地
- Culturally 文化上地
- Economically 經濟地
- Ethically 倫理上地
- Financially 財務上地
- Geographically 地理學地
- Geologically 地質學地
- Intellectually 智力上地
- Legally 法律地
- Linguistically 語言學地
- Logically 邏輯上地

- Mechanically 機械方面地
- Medically 醫學上地
- Morally 道德上地
- Physically 身體上地
- Politically 政治上
- Psychologically 心理上地
- Religiously 宗教地
- Scientifically 科學地
- Socially 社會地
- Spiritually 精神上地
- Statistically 統計上地
- Technically 技術上地

簡報時，有時候會不想用太過明顯的方式直述論點，這時可以用更**概略性的用語**（general context）替代，可以介紹較大的主題，或改寫簡報所列出的論點。你可以用「**generally speaking . . .**」這類的句型開展句子。

④ **Generally speaking**, the people are disgusted with the leadership.

大致而言，人民對他們的領導者很反感。

⑤ **Broadly speaking**, he has had a very successful career.

大體來說，他擁有一個很成功的事業。

⑥ **Superficially speaking**, the impact didn't cause any harm, but there might be internal damage.

表面上，這個衝擊沒有造成任何影響，但可能會替內部帶來損害。

除了「generally speaking . . .」，也可以用其他方式表示。

⑦ **Basically**, our current level of consumption and waste is unsustainable.

基本上，就目前我們消耗與濫用的程度看來，是無法維持下去的。

⑧ **Fundamentally**, environmentalism is about thinking globally and acting locally.

基本上，環保的概念是以全球作思維、以地方作行動。

⑨ **Essentially**, the theory states that observers in uniform motion relative to one another cannot determine if one of them is stationary.

實質上，這個理論說明了在等速運動下，觀察者相對於另一名觀察者，無法判定哪一個人是絕對的靜止。

EXAMPLES

 42

① **Doctor**

Medically speaking, smoking is not a good idea.
就醫學觀點來說，抽菸是不好的。

② **Lawyer**

Legally speaking, you can't seek custody of the children unless you have a higher income.
就法律上而言，若沒有更高的收入是無法爭取監護權的。

③ **Geologist**

Geologically speaking, those rocks tell an interesting story about Earth's natural history.
就地質學而言，那些石頭能顯示地球自然史上重要的一頁。

④ **Linguist**

Linguistically speaking, Italian is a member of the Romance group of the Italic subfamily of Indo-European languages.
就語言學而言，義大利文隸屬於印歐語系的羅曼語族。

⑤ **Theologian**

Theologically speaking, there are some fundamental differences between Sunni and Shi'ite interpretations of the Koran.
就神學而言，遜尼派和什葉派對於可蘭經的詮釋有基本上的差異。

⑥ **Banker**

Financially speaking, you would be safer to invest your savings in an Registered Retirement Savings Plan.
就財務來說，將你的儲蓄轉為退休儲蓄計劃是最安全的作法。

⑦ **Scientist**

Scientifically speaking, the theory hasn't been proven in the laboratory yet.
就科學而言，這項理論仍未經實驗證實。

⑧ **Mechanic**

Mechanically speaking, your car is fine. The damage is only cosmetic.
根據機械的觀點，你的車況良好，損傷只限表面而已。

⑨ **Politician**

Politically speaking, the senator has lost credibility with the voters because he tried to cover up the scandal.
就政治上來說，該參議員因試圖隱瞞醜聞，已失去了選民的信任。

⑩ **Basketball Coach**

Physically speaking, he's the tallest, strongest member of the team, but his contribution isn't great.
就外型而言，他是該隊最高大強壯的隊員，但他對球隊的貢獻卻十分有限。

3 Sentence qualifier phrases 修飾片語

修飾片語（qualifier phrase）由「一個介系詞 + 一個形容詞」組成，用於連結主要論點和其相關背景。句型結構包含兩組句子——第一句論述重點，而第二句具體呈現觀點。

① This year's harvest will fall far short of our expectations. **At least** we still have the government subsidy to fall back on.

今年的收成會遠低於我們所預期，但**至少**我們仍能仰賴政府的補助金。

② This year's harvest will fall far short of our expectations. **In general**, we will be in the same position we were in after last year's failed crop.

今年的收成會遠低於我們所預期。**大致說來**，我們將會面臨去年作物欠收的相同情況。

③ This year's harvest will fall far short of our expectations. **On average**, each acre will produce only 20 percent of its potential.

今年的收成會遠低於我們所預期。**平均來說**，每一英畝地只能收成 20% 的預期產量。

④ The new machinery is working well. **As things stand**, we've doubled our productivity.

新機器運作良好，**在這狀況下**，我們將能提升兩倍的生產力。

⑤ We'll have to pay additional shipping costs. **For the time being**, we're able to afford them, but they may be a problem later.

我們必須支付額外的運費。**在短期內**我們還有能力支付，但日後會有困難。

⑥ They want to cancel the project. **In some respects,** it has been successful, but overall it has been far too costly.

他們想取消這項計劃。**由某些層面看來**，這計劃還算成功，但整體而言仍然要價昂貴。

⑦ They're asking far too much for the repair. **On no account** should we pay that price.

他們的賠償要求太過分了，**不管怎樣**我們都不會支付該金額的。

⑧ Their offer is complicated. **On the face of** it, the offer looks extremely attractive, but we'll lose our leading position in the industry.

這項提案太複雜了，**表面上**很誘人，但我們會失去在此產業的領先優勢。

162

⑨ Our competitive advantage has been lost. **For now,** we're still profitable, but that won't last much longer.

我們已失去競爭優勢，**現在**雖然仍有盈收，但這情況不會再持續太久。

⑩ We will try to keep our pricing competitive. **Under no circumstances**, though, can we survive a price war with such a large company.

我們會保持價格的競爭力，但**不管如何**，要在價格戰上打贏如此大的公司是不可能的。

⑪ It's just a matter of time before we succeed. **At present**, we need to keep working hard to meet our third-quarter goals.

勝利就在不遠處，**目前**我們得繼續努力好達到第三季的目標。

⑫ Government regulation has provided stability. **Up to a point**, this kind of intervention is bad, but it has made some things more predictable.

政府規條能提供穩定性，**在一定程度上**，政府的干預會有負面影響，但這也讓一些事物更有可預期性。

⑬ The takeover won't affect your salaries. **At the most**, you'll have to put in a little overtime in the first month.

這項併購案並不會影響你的薪資，**最差的狀況**是你在整併的第一個月也許要加班。

⑭ We'll deliver the new cars in February. **Until then**, I'm sure you'll appreciate the added exercise you get from walking.

我們將會在二月時交車，**在那之前**，我想你會很享受走路這項額外的運動。

⑮ We'll see what happens before they declare bankruptcy. **As a last resort,** they might still try to blackmail us.

我們會觀察他們宣布破產的情況，**最糟的狀況**是他們可能會持續勒索我們。

⑯ The weather was ideal last year. **Under the right conditions**, our soybeans should thrive again this year.

去年天氣極佳，**在良好的狀況下**，今年黃豆應該也會生產良好。

⑰ My subject today is the volatility of the market. **On the whole**, I believe you're all familiar with the background information.

我今日的主題是市場的反覆無常，**大體而言**，我想你們都對此主題有相當的背景知識。

UNIT 18

Making a Point With a Rhetorical Question
用疑問帶出主題重點

以**反詰**方式提出論點,能鼓勵聽眾對其答案進行評論性的思考。

1. PowerPoint slide → Question → Answer 投影片介紹 → 提問 → 給予回答
2. Statement → Question → Answer 陳述簡報要點 → 提問 → 給予回答

演説者在簡報時提出問題,不一定要獲得聽眾的解答,卻可以激發聽眾思考。

★ 在簡報中,你可以**直接回答自己提出的問題**:

Our marketing plan for this extraordinary product is just not working.
➤ So what's the problem?
➤ Well, the problem is poor communication between the designers and the marketing team.

我們對於這項特別產品的行銷策略成效不佳。
➤ 那麼,問題的癥結在哪裡?
➤ 這個嘛,設計者和行銷小組間的溝通出了問題。

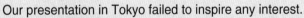
★ 也可以讓答案顯而易見的問題醞釀並發揮效應,之後再**補充背景資料和相關資訊**:

Our presentation in Tokyo failed to inspire any interest.
➤ So what happened?
➤ Well, let us go back to the beginning for a moment . . .

我們在東京的簡報並未引起任何迴響。
➤ 所以,出了什麼問題呢?
➤ 這個嘛,我們先從一開始説起……

★ 在簡報時**開展反詰句**的兩種方式：

1 PowerPoint slide → Question → Answer
投影片介紹 → 提問 → 給予回答

直接問題需要一個**直接答案**（direct answer），回答問題時，答案必須要使用和提問相同的字詞，像是「**problem**」和「**the problem is . . .**」。

> 直接答案

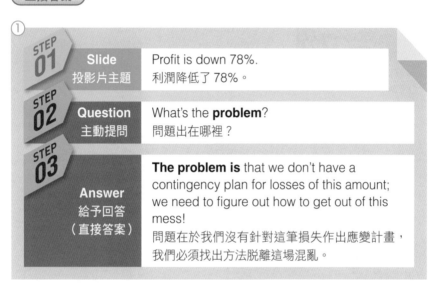

①

STEP 01	Slide 投影片主題	Profit is down 78%. 利潤降低了 78%。
STEP 02	Question 主動提問	What's the **problem**? 問題出在哪裡？
STEP 03	Answer 給予回答（直接答案）	**The problem is** that we don't have a contingency plan for losses of this amount; we need to figure out how to get out of this mess! 問題在於我們沒有針對這筆損失作出應變計畫，我們必須找出方法脫離這場混亂。

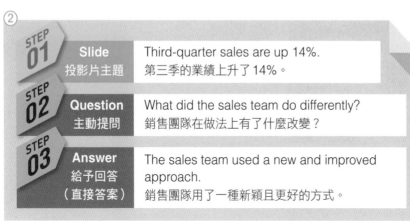

②

STEP 01	Slide 投影片主題	Third-quarter sales are up 14%. 第三季的業績上升了 14%。
STEP 02	Question 主動提問	What did the sales team do differently? 銷售團隊在做法上有了什麼改變？
STEP 03	Answer 給予回答（直接答案）	The sales team used a new and improved approach. 銷售團隊用了一種新穎且更好的方式。

③

STEP 01	**Slide** 投影片主題	Our company's market share this year is lower than last year's share. 公司今年的市占率比去年還低。
STEP 02	**Question** 主動提問	What has been the biggest effect? 這對公司最大的影響為何？
STEP 03	**Answer** 給予回答 （直接答案）	The biggest effect is that we lost our position as the largest PC manufacturer. 最大的影響是我們失掉桌上型電腦的龍頭地位。

　　有些提問本身就有直接答案，這種情況下，反詰句後面應該加上一個**間接答案**（indirect answer），不直接回應問題，反而以其他不相關的資訊回答。

間接答案

④

STEP 01	**Slide** 投影片主題	Profit is down 78%. 利潤降低了 78%。
STEP 02	**Question** 主動提問	Why are we continuing with this venture if we're not making any money? 在無法獲利的情形下，為什麼我們還要繼續投資這項事業？
STEP 03	**Answer** 給予回答 （間接答案）	We should liquidate as much remaining product as we can and cut our losses. 我們應該清算剩餘的產品，並且減少目前的損失。

⑤

STEP 01	**Slide** 投影片主題	Profit is down 78%. 利潤降低了 78%。
STEP 02	**Question** 主動提問	How could we let this happen? 這樣的情況為什麼會發生？
STEP 03	**Answer** 給予回答 （間接答案）	If we don't quit now and cut our losses, we'll be bankrupt by February. 如果我們現在不中止，並且減少目前的損失，我們到二月就會破產了。

⑥

STEP 01	**Slide** 投影片主題	Profit is down 78%. 利潤降低了 78%。
STEP 02	**Question** 主動提問	Has our profitability ever been this low? 過去我們的獲利率也曾經那麼低落嗎？
STEP 03	**Answer** 給予回答 （間接答案）	We should dissolve the company ASAP! 我們應該盡快解散公司！

2 Statement → Question → Answer
陳述簡報要點 → 提問 → 給予回答

　　在簡報進行的任何階段，都可以**先陳述簡報要點，再提出疑問，並給予回答**。與上述「使用投影片介紹主題」不同的是，你會將簡報主題以**口述**的方式向聽眾講解。此外，大部分這類型的簡報陳述，需要用「**so**」當作句子的開頭。

★ **Indirect Answer** 間接答案　｜　以其他相關資訊婉轉地陳述，回答時使用和問題同樣的**名詞**和**動詞**。

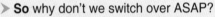

Changing over to a supplier with a proven reputation abroad is essential for improving our reliability.

➤ **So** why don't we switch over ASAP?
➤ We all know that the longer we delay the change, the more money we will lose.

改與享譽海外的供應商合作，可以改善我們的可靠度。

➤ **所以**為什麼我們不盡早更換合作廠商？
➤ 我們都清楚知道，更換廠商的時間拖越久，浪費的資金也就越多。

★ **Direct Answer** 直接答案　｜　答案本身直截了當

The financial trouble we're in now can be overcome.

➤ So what's the solution?
➤ **The solution** is to downsize immediately.

現在我們面臨的財政危機是可以被克服的。

➤ 所以解決方法為何？
➤ **解決方法**是立刻裁員。

某些英文的詰問句因為經常被使用而成為**慣用語**。
下列反詰句具備慣用語句的特色，而且多半後面都接**間接答案**。

① What are we waiting for?　我們還在等什麼？
（我們趕快開始吧！）

② What are the chances?　機會有多大？

③ What's next?　接下來呢？

④ What's the point?　重點是？

⑤ What's up? / What's up with that?　出了什麼差錯？

⑥ What's the deal? / What's the deal with that?　發生什麼事了？

⑦ What did you expect?　你期待什麼？

⑧ Where did we go wrong?　是哪裡出了問題呢？

⑨ Who cares?　誰在乎啊？

⑩ Who do they think they're kidding?　他們以為在騙誰？

⑪ Are you kidding me?　你在開玩笑吧？

⑫ Are you serious?　你說真的嗎？

⑬ Isn't that ironic?　這不是很諷刺嗎？

⑭ Isn't that interesting?　這不是很有趣嗎？

⑮ Need I say more?　還需要我再多說什麼嗎？

Indirect Answer 間接答案

In China, there is a huge demand right now for our product.

➤ So what are we waiting for?
➤ Let's get the distribution channels established immediately.

① ....

目前我們商品在中國的需求量很高。

➤ 所以我們還在等什麼？
➤ 我們得立刻建立銷售通路。

As this graph shows, our company is becoming more and more recognizable abroad.

➤ So isn't this what we were hoping for?
➤ We applied the market research, and it paid off.

② ....

圖表顯示我們公司在國外的知名度越來越高。

➤ 所以這不就是我們所期望的目標嗎？
➤ 我們的市場調查發揮作用了。

This latest offer is ridiculously low.

➤ So are they serious?
➤ We can't even begin to consider the deal at that price.

③ ....

最新的交易報價不可思議的低。

➤ 他們是認真的嗎？
➤ 這樣的價格讓我們根本不該去考慮接受這個提案。

B Direct Answer 直接答案

At the beginning, the buyer was totally committed, but then things changed.

➤ So what happened?
➤ It's simple. What happened is the deal fell through because the buyer's financial backer decided to back somebody else.

④

起初，買家對案子很熱衷，但後來一切卻走了樣。

➤ 發生了什麼事？
➤ 很簡單，這場交易失敗的原因是因為買家的投資者決定轉投資別人。

We are still unable to get solid footing in the American market.

➤ So what's the problem?
➤ Well, I think the problem is underexposure of the product. The scope of the advertising campaign is too small.

⑤

我們仍無法在美國市場佔有一席之地。

➤ 問題出在哪裡？
➤ 我認為問題出在產品的低曝光率，我們的廣告宣傳規模太小了。

Let's move on to our plan for this year's conference.

➤ What is our primary objective?
➤ Well, the most important objective is to have a high percentage of online sales.

⑥

讓我們來討論今年的研討會計劃。

➤ 我們主要的目標是什麼？
➤ 最重要的目標是創造高網路銷售量。

Addressing the Audience
對觀眾直述重點

如果你能讓聽眾有參與感，就能增加成功傳達訊息的機會。

除了使用反詰問句吸引觀眾注意，另一種方法就是**直接對聽眾直述論點**。

① **I'm sure you'll all agree that** we must make more sales in Asia next year.

我確定你們都將同意我們明年必須在亞洲達到更好的業績。

② **I'm confident you'll all concur that** an increase in productivity is essential.

我確信你們都會同意提升生產力是極為重要的。

③ **I think you all realize that** the modifications aren't necessarily permanent.

我相信你們都了解這個修正不一定是固定不變的。

④ **I believe you all understand** the basics of the theory.

我相信你們都了解此理論的基本概念。

⑤ **Some of you may already know** about next year's target.

有些人可能已經知道了明年的目標。

⑥ **Some of you might be aware** that layoffs are coming.

有些人可能已經知道我們即將會裁員。

⑦ **If you haven't** read Dr. Rick Black's study, **I suggest you do so**.

如果你還沒讀過瑞克‧布雷克博士的著作，**我建議你可以看看**。

⑧ **If you aren't familiar with** the report, **I recommend** reading it.

若你還不熟悉這份報告，**我建議**你們讀一讀。

Listing Points
列出要點

將簡報論點列出來,可以讓聽眾跟上你的腳步,並且更加清楚了解你的重點。
你可以藉由向聽眾發出信號(signal),來表示你即將要進行的簡報方向。

1. General items to be discussed 概略性重點討論
2. Options, advantages, and disadvantages 選擇、優點與缺點

　　通常演說或報告的開頭,就會先分項列出要點,讓聽眾明白簡報的整體結構。**條列式整理出重點**,會加速簡報進行的有效程度,幫助解釋不同論點。

1 General items to be discussed 概略性重點討論

　　簡報中任何需要討論的事項,無論描述不同的種類、某項提案的主旨、長期的發展,或是進行程序的步驟等,都可以藉由**分項列點的方法**,和聽眾進行更明確的溝通,不用一開始就急著針對某個論點展開論述。

①**轉折語**:then、next、after that

你可以用**序數**進行分項,或是利用 then、next、after that 這些單字來介紹。

① There are **two** types of buyers that we have to think about: buyers who identify strongly with brand names and buyers who are looking for high performance, no matter what the brand.

我們必須納入考慮**兩種**類型的顧客:偏好名牌的顧客與注重產品效能而非品牌的顧客。

Let's look at **each of these** types in more detail.

讓我們更深入檢視**這兩種**類型的顧客。

First off, there are the brand name buyers. They . . .

首先是偏好名牌的顧客。他們……

Next, there are the performance-minded buyers. Their . . .

接著是注重產品效能的顧客。他們的……

(2) 條列語：first、firstly、to start with

(2) Let's examine the production cost **first**. The cost of . . .

首先，我們來檢視價格。價錢是……。

The second thing to consider is property tax. The rate is . . .

第二則是考慮房地產稅。現在的稅率是……

Third, there's insurance. It's essential, and . . .

第三是保險。保險是必要的，而且……

(3) 反詰句：利用問句列舉論點

(3) **Can we really expect to meet the deadline?** Absolutely! Let me tell you how: **first, by** hiring two new marketing writers, **then by** outsourcing the technical manuals, **and finally by** limiting the number of requests from the notebook division. Now, let's look at each of these ideas in more detail.

我們真能如期完成嗎？當然沒問題。我來告訴你訣竅，**首先**，多請兩位行銷文案撰稿員，**然後**將維修技術手冊外包，**而最後**再控制筆電部門的要求量。現在讓我們更加深入探討這些論點。

(4) **Is this a realistic proposal?** No way! Let me put it this way: The distribution **is wrong**, the marketing **is wrong**, and the profit margin **is wrong**. Now let's look at each of these problems in more detail.

這是一個實際可行的企劃案嗎？這是行不通的！我換個方式跟你說好了。產品分配**出錯**，行銷企劃**不能採用**，而毛利率**也有問題**。現在讓我們一一深入探討這些論點。

④ 強調語：especially

使用**簡潔有力的回答方式加強語氣**，增加簡報效果。在這狀況下，「especially」
是個很好用的字彙。

⑤ Where is business really booming? Alberta. In Edmonton and
especially in Calgary.

我們的生意在哪裡最成功？亞伯達省。在埃德蒙頓，**特別在**卡加立最能成功。

⑥ Can we improve the procedure? Definitely! In terms of quality, in terms
of quantity, and **especially** in terms of speed.

我們能改善工作程序嗎？當然可以！在品質、產量和**尤其是**速度方面都能
改善。

EXAMPLES

Ⓐ 條列語

①   I'm going to be showing you five examples from around the
world. First, I'll show you an example from Sri Lanka and then a
second example from Tanzania. Third, I'll show you an American
sample, and the fourth one will be from Mexico. The final example will
be from China. OK, let's get started with Sri Lanka. When you look
closely at this example, you can see . . .

現在我要帶你看來自世界各地的五個例子。首先是斯里蘭卡，接著是坦尚尼
亞。第三要看的是美國，然後第四是墨西哥，最後則是中國。好，現在要從
斯里蘭卡開始講起，當你仔細看過這個地區，你會發現⋯⋯

②   I'll be discussing several crucial tasks involved in the growth
cycle of a successful crop. To start, you must germinate the
seeds. Then you have to monitor their development, separate the
males from the females as early as possible, water, fertilize, and prune
the plants as required, harvest the plants at the right time, and finally

dry and cure the product properly. All right? So, I'll begin with the germination process . . .

我接下來要進行一些關於優良作物成長周期的重要討論。首先,你必須播種,接著,你得監控其生長過程、提早分枝雄株和雌株、灌溉、施肥及修剪雜枝雜葉、及時 收割,並且在最後的步驟進行徹底的產品乾燥。沒問題了嗎?那麼,我將會從生長過程開始講述……

(B) 反詰句

③ **How is the reorganization of the European department working out?** Quite well, as you'll see! First, communication is improving. Second, sales are up. Third, profits are soaring!

歐洲部門的重組成效如何?還不錯。第一,溝通變得更有效率;第二,業績上升;第三,利潤飆升。

④ **What does a reliable supplier mean at this point?** It means more of everything: more predictability, more sales, more profit.

在這個狀況,可靠的供應商代表什麼?代表一切都將更好。更高的預期性,更多業績和更多利潤。

⑤ **Would changing management at this juncture affect us?** No doubt about it! There would be fewer employees, fewer clients, and less reliability.

在這情況中改組管理階層會對我們造成影響嗎?當然會!員工會更少、客戶流失、信賴度也會降低。

⑥ **Is advertising absolutely essential for us?** Not necessarily. Look at Starbucks, look at Avon, and especially look at Google.

廣告行銷對我們真有那麼重要嗎?其實不然。看看星巴克、雅芳,特別是谷歌就知道了。

2 Options, advantages, and disadvantages
選擇、優點與缺點

① **兩種選擇**

要列出未來企業可能的發展選擇，需要提出可供參考的行動方針。

① There are **two ways to go** on this issue. **One way** is to set up a second facility in the science park right away. **The other** is to wait until next year and add a new wing onto the existing factory site.

對於這個問題有**兩種可行的做法**：**第一**是立刻在科學園區設立第二座工廠；**另一個**是等到明年，在現在工廠的位址旁加建廠房。

② **Two possible options are open** to us at this point. **First**, we could . . . **On the other hand**, we could . . .

現在這個時候有**兩種選擇可考慮**。**一方面**，我們可以……，**另一方面**我們能……。

② **多種選擇**

③ There are **a number of options available** at the moment. Let me explain them one by one.

現在我們有**許多選擇**，讓我一一來介紹。

首 先

④ **To begin with**, we could . . .　　首先我們可以……

⑤ **For starters**, we could . . .　　一開始我們可以……

⑥ **One thing** we could do is . . .　　我們能做的**一件事**是……

178

次者

⑦ **Another thing** we could do is . . .　　　另一個我們可以做的是……

⑧ **Another angle** would be to . . .　　　從**另一個角度**來看……

再者

⑨ **Otherwise**, we could . . .　　　不然，我們得……

⑩ **Instead**, we could . . .　　　取而代之，我們……

結語

⑪ **Alternatively**, we could . . .　　　另一種方式是，我們……

⑫ **As a last resort**, we could . . .　　　作為最終手段，我們……

⑬ **If all else fails**, we could . . .　　　若其他的方法都無效，我們就……

③ 複合

當你想要討論某項選擇、策略或主題的多重優點和缺點，可以使用以下句型：

⑭ We have identified **four advantages** and **two disadvantages** to this strategy. Let me outline the advantages first.

　我們發現此策略中有**四項優點**以及**兩項缺點**。我先就優勢部分做介紹。

➤ **One is** . . .　　　　　　➤ 一項是……
➤ **Another is** . . .　　　　➤ 另一項為……
➤ **A third advantage is** . . .　➤ 第三項優點是……
➤ **Finally**, . . .　　　　　　➤ 最後則為……

⑮ OK. So now let's turn to the disadvantages.

　好，現在我們來檢視它的缺點。

➤ **First**, . . .　　　　　　➤ 第一……
➤ **Second**, . . .　　　　　➤ 第二……

179

如果描述優勢和劣勢的**句子都不長**，也不需要詳加解釋，你可以用以下的範例**直接表達**：

⑯ The advantages are that raw materials are cheaper, labor is more abundant, and the production facility requires only minor modifications.

優勢在於原料價格便宜、勞力充足，而生產設備只需要些微調整。

⑰ The disadvantages are the distance from the market and the currency risk.

劣勢為距離市場較遠與匯率風險。

要解決以上情形，可採取三點行動方針：

⑱ Well, for the first one . . .　　　　　嗯，從第一點看來……

⑲ The second . . .　　　　　　　　　　第二點……

⑳ Finally, for the third one . . .　　　　最後第三點……

反詰句

㉑ **What options are available to us now?** Basically, there are two: We could hire temporary replacement workers and operate at half speed, or we could accept the union's terms and be back to full-capacity production next week.

現在我們有什麼選擇？基本上有兩種：我們可以先雇用約聘替代勞工，減半產能；或者我們可以接受工會的條件，從下星期開始恢復正常產量。

EXAMPLES

① 　Two things related to the product line require in-depth discussion. **The first** is design. **The second** is quality.

我們的產品線有兩點需要深入的討論，第一是設計，第二是品質。

② 　There are two possibilities for us to consider. **On the one hand**, we could wait them out. **On the other hand**, we could force the issue right now.

有兩種可以考慮的可能性，一方面，我們可以等待他們，另一方面，我們可以要求他們立即處理。

③ 　What options are on the table for us at this point? Well, **first off**, we could sue the company. **Alternatively**, we could force the issue right now.

在這個情況下我們有什麼選擇？第一，我們可以控告該公司，或是我們也可以要求他們立即著手處理。

④ 　Let me break down the pros and cons. The main advantage is that the clothes become cleaner. The disadvantages include more wear on the clothes.

讓我分析一下優缺點。主要的優點是讓衣服更乾淨，缺點則包含高耗損率。

⑤ 　A few possibilities are available at the moment. Let me explain them one by one. **One thing** we could do is get low-interest loans and try to buy and sell as many properties as we can. **Another thing** to do would be to liquidate our assets and invest the capital. **As a last resort**, we may have to declare bankruptcy.

現在我們有一些選擇，讓我一一介紹。首先我們可以申請低利率貸款並盡可能地買賣房地產，另一種方式是清算我們的資產並做投資，而最不得已的手段是宣告破產。

UNIT 21 Listing Points in a Specific Sequence
列出要點的順序

列出要點清單的技巧在於運用特別用語（wording），將每個要點依照特定順序（sequence）排放。

1. Logical progression 邏輯進程
2. Time series 時間序列
3. Compare and contrast 比較與對照
4. Problems and solutions 問題與解答
5. Inductive and deductive reasoning 歸納法與演繹法
6. Building up to a point you support/oppose 將論點歸結至贊成或反對的立場

1 Logical progression 邏輯進程

① 進程語（1）：序數

① Successfully starting a business involves **three essential steps**: **one**, monitoring the market; **two**, defining the criteria for success; **three**, determining how to stick to those criteria over the long term.

要成功創業需要**三項必要步驟**：一、監督市場；二、確立成功的標準；三、擁有「長期遵循成功標準」的決心。

② Optimizing your website is actually a **two-part process**: **First**, you have to optimize programming during the development phase; **then**, you need to focus on post-development functioning, which is equally critical.

有兩個部分可以提高你網站的效能：**第一**、在開發時加強程式設計，**然後**繼續致力提升開發後的網站品質，這點十分重要。

② 進程語（2）：**start with → move on → end with**

③ Let me outline the factory's production cycle. It **starts with** intake and storage; **moves on**, to preparation, assembly, and packaging; **and ends with** distribution.

讓我向你解釋我們工廠的生產循環。**首先**它會先引進並儲存原料；**接著**開始準備生產線與進行包裝；**最後**才是產品分配發售。

③ 進程語（3）：**begin with → move through → finish with**

④ The documentation process has three stages. It **begins with** the writing phase, **moves through** the editing stage, and **finishes with** the layout and design work.

文件產製過程包含三個步驟。**首先**是撰稿，**再進展**到文章編輯階段，**最後是**版面編排與整體設計。

④ 較長的進程語

⑤ There are six stages to the process: 　　整個過程有六個階段：

> First, . . . 　　　　　　　　　　　　　> 第一……
> Then, . . . 　　　　　　　　　　　　　> 接著……
> After that, . . . 　　　　　　　　　　> 在……之後是
> Then (x), . . . 　　　　　　　　　　　> 然後是（x）
> After (x), . . . there's (y) . . . 　　　> （x）之後是（y）……
> Lastly, . . . 　　　　　　　　　　　　> 最後……

EXAMPLE 53

Website Development

1 understanding your objectives
2 content management
3 site map
4 content formatting for search engine visibility
5 editing
6 publishing

There are six stages to the process: **First**, you have to understand your objectives. **After that**, there's content management **and then** development of the site map. **After** the site map is done, there's content formatting for search engine visibility and editing. **Lastly**, there's publishing.

架設網站有六個階段。你必須先了解網站的目的，接著要研擬內容，規劃網站地圖。等到網站地圖確定後，要設立方便搜尋引擎搜尋的內容樣式，並加以編輯，最後網站才能上線啟用。

2 Time series 時間序列

 54

　　演講時，有時你會想以特定的時間架構來列舉一連串的事件。讓某些事情按照**時間順序**（chronological order）來排列，或是更換事物順序，來加強它在某個時間點上的重要性。

① Let me describe the development of the idea. **First, I'll talk about** the background, **then** the present situation, and **then** the prospects for the future.

　　我來解釋一下這個概念的發展。**首先我會談論**其背景資訊，**接著**是目前的情形，**然後**是未來的展望。

....

　　若想要比較過去和現在的發展，並強調**過去**的狀況，你可以這樣排列句子：

② **In the beginning**, the retail outlets were extremely successful. **Recently**, however, they haven't been very profitable.

　　起初，零售店大獲成功，但是**近來**零售店的利潤卻不太好。

③ **When we started**, Web-based advertising didn't exist; **nowadays** it comprises 75% of our marketing budget.

　　我們創業時，網路廣告的行銷方式尚未出現，**但最近**它占據了我們 75% 的行銷費用。

④ **At first**, the hotel's restaurant wasn't great, **but as of late**, with the new management, it's really improved.

　　一開始，飯店餐廳的評價不佳，**但近來**因新式管理奏效，已經有明顯改善。

若想要比較過去和現在的發展，並**強調現在狀況**，你可以這樣排列句子：

⑤ **At present**, we're already seeing a huge improvement **over last year**. At this moment in time, growth has already made us more profitable than last year. This year's bonus will depend on your performance **throughout the past year**.

目前我們已經觀察到**去年**的大幅進步，而目前的獲利比去年成長更多，今年的分紅獎金將由你**去年一整年**的表現決定。

你也可以依照過去或現在的經驗，強調**未來**會發生的事件。

⑥ **In the years to come**, we'll have to be mindful of the lessons we learned **last year**.

在未來幾年，我們必須謹記在**去年**學到的寶貴經驗。

⑦ **Next year's** outlook can't be estimated **until this year's** figures are compiled.

想預測**明年的**展望，必須要**等到今年的**數據資料出爐。

更多時間短語

起初
- originally
- in the beginning

過去
- throughout last year
- during the previous year
- previously this year
- earlier in the year

近來
- recently
- lately

現在
- at present
- right now
- currently
- as of right now
- at this moment in time
- at the moment
- as it stands now

未來
- eventually
- in the future

3 Compare and contrast 比較與對照 (55)

★ **比較**是檢視事物的**相似性**，而**對照**是檢視其**相異處**。

① The technologies **work similarly, but they are also unique** in some significant ways. I'll explain the similarities first. To begin with, . . .

這些技術**大同小異**，但卻也有許多**大相逕庭**之處。我先解釋它們的相似點。首先⋯⋯

② His methods are **quite similar** to ours; however, **there are some crucial differences**. First, I'll outline the things we have in common. For starters, . . .

他的方法**和**我們的**很相似**，但是**某些部分卻截然不同**。首先，我會先介紹這些方法的共通點⋯⋯

③ There is **some likeness** between them, but there are also **significant variations**. Let's go over the similarities. Firstly, . . .

兩者有些**相似處**，但仍然有**極大的**差異。我們先從相同的地方開始談。首先是⋯⋯

★ 強調事物的**相似處**。

④ There are a number of **similarities between the two** proposals. First, . . .

這**兩個**提案有幾個**相似之處**。首先是⋯⋯

⑤ The three experiments **share** five **remarkable traits**. First, . . .

這三個實驗**有**五處**相同的卓越特徵**。首先是⋯⋯

★ 強調事物的**不同點**。

⑥ Our product **differs from** theirs in four ways. First, . . .

我們的產品有四點**和**他們的**不同**。第一⋯⋯

⑦ **There are several key differences in the responses** of rural and urban residents. I'll read the rural ones first, . . .

城鄉居民分別**出現了一些不同的反應**。我先從鄉下居民的回應開始唸⋯⋯

187

4 Problems and solutions 問題與解答

簡報的重點通常在於**列出問題並給予解答**。你可以練習使用下列範例來列舉問題、提供解決辦法。

① **The problem is financing.** If we look at the long term, we will definitely need more financial support.

問題在於財政。如果長遠來看，我們絕對需要更多的財政資助。

你也可以使用**反詰句**提問並解答：

② The problem is financing. If we look at the long term, we will definitely need more financial support. **So what's the solution?** Well, I suggest we sell the property in Tianmu.

問題在於財政。如果長遠來看，我們絕對需要更多的財務資源。所以，解決辦法為何？嗯……我想我們可以將天母的房子售出。

你也可能要**針對單一問題給予多重解答**：

③ **Our number one obstacle this year** was the troublesome government intervention. I'd like to propose two possible solutions.

我們今年最大的阻礙是政府的干預，在這邊我想提出兩種可行的解決方案。

First, we could . . .

第一，我們可以……

The other solution would be to . . .

另一個方法是……

你也會遇到更複雜的問題，需要**提出許多解決方法**：

④ **The difficulties** experienced last quarter in sales include poor organization, poor communication, and underfunding. Is there a quick fix to all these problems? Not really. Let me explain **each** problem **in turn** and propose solutions for each one. OK. **First, regarding the organizational challenges,** . . .

上一季我們在銷售上遇到的**各種困難**包括：缺乏完善組織、溝通不良，以及資金不足。針對這些問題是否有快速的解決方案？沒有。我將**逐一介紹各項**問題及它們的解決辦法。好，**首先是組織不夠完善這點**……

- -

另一種可能的情況是，**許多問題都指向同一個解決方案**：

⑤ **There are four quite serious problems to be considered:** First, a huge crack in the foundation; second, leaks in the roof; third, the worn-out window seals; and fourth, the pit of quicksand in the backyard. **The best solution to all these problems is** to look for a new house.

有四項較重大的問題要納入考慮：第一、地基出現裂縫；第二、屋頂的漏水情況；第三、窗戶封條磨損，以及第四、在後院的流沙坑。**以上最好的解決方法**就是另外找間房子吧。

EXAMPLE Ⓐ

① Low morale among staff members has become a real problem. The solution? I suggest we have an all-expenses-paid company cocktail party.

員工士氣不振已成為嚴重的問題。解決方式？我建議公司辦一場免費的雞尾酒派對。

Problem Low morale among staff members
員工士氣不振

Solution Have an all-expenses-paid company cocktail party
辦一場免費的雞尾酒派對

EXAMPLE Ⓑ

② There have been a lot of complaints about late shipments. I'd like to propose two courses of action to solve this problem: First, we call a meeting with the shipping department; second, we give partial refunds to customers who have complained.

我們收到許多針對出貨延誤的客訴，我想要提出兩項行動建議以解決問題。第一、我們可以與貨運公司開會協談；第二、對於提出客訴的客戶，我們可以給予部分退費賠償。

Problem A lot of complaints about late shipments
收到許多針對出貨延誤的客訴

Solution Call a meeting with the shipping department; give partial refunds to customers who have complained
與貨運公司開會協談，並對於提出客訴的客戶給予部分退費賠償

EXAMPLE C

③   A few problems have to be taken care of: For starters, there are too many cooks in the kitchen. Next, there are not enough cooking utensils. Finally, a lot of outdated equipment is constantly in need of repair. The best solution to all these problems is to totally remodel the kitchen.

    我們有許多問題需要處理：第一、廚房內的廚師太多；第二、烹飪用具不夠；最後，有許多老舊的設備常常需要修繕。最好的解決方式是將廚房進行大規模的整修。

Problem
Too many cooks in the kitchen; not enough cooking utensils; outdated equipment that is constantly in need of repair
廚房內的廚師太多、烹飪用具不夠、有許多老舊的設備常常需要修繕

Solution
Remodel the kitchen
整修廚房

Deductive reasoning 演繹法

處理簡報中**廣泛被接受的經驗事實或資料**（empirical facts or data），可以使用演繹法。**演繹法**（deductive reasoning）所陳述的是肯定的事實，意思就是當你以此方法為論據時，你相信它所呈現的證據能充分支持其假設（premise），而推論出來的結果將會完全無誤。

假設 ①

Premise A	All men are mortal.	所有人類都是凡人。
Premise B	Socrates was a man.	蘇格拉底是人類。
Conclusion	Therefore, Socrates was mortal.	因此，蘇格拉底是凡人。
① In presentation	**Because** all men are mortal and Socrates was a man, **we can certainly assume** he was mortal, too.	由於所有人類都是凡人，蘇格拉底是人類，**所以我們可認定**蘇格拉底**一定**是凡人。

以上的假設與結論中，重複使用的字（man、mortal、Socrates、was）和 therefore（所以）這個連接詞，經常在邏輯推理或更正式的情境下使用——用兩組假設和一個結論形成一套標準演繹法。

假設 ②

Premise A	The latest technology always sells well.	搭配最新科技的產品總是能創下銷售佳績。
Premise B	This technology is the latest.	這項產品擁有最新科技。
Conclusion	Therefore, this technology will sell well.	所以這項科技產品將賣得很好。
② In presentation	**By virtue of the fact that** the latest technology always sells well, **we can definitely expect** our newest offering to also do well.	由於搭配最新科技的產品有好的銷售成績，**我們可以預期**我們的最新產品也會賣得很好。

假設 ③

Premise A	There are fire ants in this shipment of hay.	這批牧草中有火蟻。
Premise B	This shipment of hay came from South America.	這批牧草來自於南美洲。
Conclusion	Therefore, all shipments of hay from South America should be checked for fire ants.	因此，所有來自南美洲的牧草應該都該被查看是否有火蟻。
③ **In presentation**	**Given that** this shipment of hay from South America contains fire ants, **we should assume that all** shipments from that continent need to be checked for ants.	**由於**這批來自南美洲的牧草中有火蟻，**我們認為所有**來自南美洲的牧草都該被查看是否有火蟻。

Inductive reasoning 歸納法

　　如果簡報中使用的消息來源不一定可靠，像是問卷調查、政治上的民意調查、焦點團體做的行銷報告，或甚至只是你自身的觀察，都可以使用**歸納法**（inductive reasoning）。

　　以歸納法作論據的假設，是用來支持某個結論的**可能事實**，它介於肯定事實和經過觀察得來的假說之間。通常由歸納法得出的結果，會拿來和演繹法的結論互相比較。

假設 ④

④		
Premise A	California is west of the Mississippi River.	加州在密西西比河的西邊。
Premise B	Texas is west of the Mississippi River.	德州在密西西比河的西邊。
Conclusion	Therefore, every city in California and Texas is west of the Mississippi River.	因此，所有在加州和德州的城市都在密西西比河的西邊。

假 設 **5**

⑤

Premise A	The poll results indicate that the president is unpopular.	民調的結果顯示這位總統不受歡迎。
Premise B	The poll results indicate that the president's opponent is well liked and respected.	民調結果表示該總統的對手大受歡迎和敬愛。
Conclusion	**Based on** the poll results, we **hypothesize** that the president will lose the next election to his opponent.	**根據**民調結果,我們可以**推測**總統大概會在下次選戰失利並輸給對手。

假 設 **6**

⑥

Premise A	Over the last few weeks, we have surveyed 100 customers who walked into our store, and 75% said they were satisfied with our inventory.	在過去幾週中,我們對 100 位來到店中的顧客做意見調查,其中有 75% 的顧客表示他們對本店的商品感到滿意。
Premise B	The 100 customers surveyed were chosen at random.	這 100 位顧客是隨機選出來的。
Probable outcomes	**Therefore**, **we can conclude that** the vast majority of people who shop in our store are satisfied with our inventory.	**因此我們認為**大多數來本店購物的顧客都對我們的商品感到滿意。

假設 **7** 提出細節

⑦			
Premise	A six-year study found that people who took a 30-minute nap at least three times a week had a 37 percent lower risk of heart-related death. Among working men, the risk was reduced by 64 percent.	一份為期六年的研究指出，一週至少三天有睡30分鐘午覺習慣的人，較一般人少37%死於心臟相關疾病的機率，尤其上班族的機率更是減少64%。	
Conclusion	Napping three times a week **may** increase your longevity.	養成午睡習慣，**可能會**增長人的壽命。	

你可以將以上例子的假設和結論互相交換，**先說結論，再談論其假設**：

⑧ A study **suggests** that napping will **likely** lengthen your life. **The six-year study found** that those who took a 30-minute nap at least three times a week had a 37 percent lower risk of heart-related death. Among working men, the risk was reduced by 64 percent.

某項研究**顯示**午睡**可能**會幫助增長你的壽命。**一份**為期六年的**研究報告指出**，一週至少有睡 三 天30分鐘午覺的人，較一般人減少37%的心臟疾病死亡率。上班族的機率更是減少64%。

其他可以形容**可能結論**的用語有：

⑨ In all likelihood, the . . .　　　　極有可能……

⑩ Perhaps the . . .　　　　　　　　也許……

⑪ It's probable that the . . .　　　　有可能是……

演繹法

A

Premise	It has snowed in Saskatchewan every December in recorded history.	歷史記載，薩斯喀徹溫省每年12月都會下雪。
Conclusion	Therefore, it will snow in Saskatchewan this coming December.	因此，今年12月薩斯喀徹溫省也會下雪。

In presentation

① Because it has snowed in Saskatchewan every December in recorded history, we can certainly expect it to snow again this year at the same time.

由於根據歷史記載，薩斯喀徹溫省每年12月都會下雪，我們可以預期今年12月薩斯喀徹溫省也會下雪。

B

Premise A	The whole market is improving.	這個市場正蓬勃發展。
Premise B	Our company deals in this market.	我們公司投入該市場。
Conclusion	Therefore, our company will improve.	因此，我們公司也將蓬勃發展。

In presentation

② Given that the whole market is improving and that our company deals in this market, it's probable that our company will improve.

由於整個市場都在蓬勃發展中，而我們公司又有投入該市場，我們公司也將可能會蓬勃發展。

歸納法

C

Premise	The study found that Internet users under the age of 30 were more likely to use wireless devices than those between the ages of 31 and 49.	研究顯示30歲以下的網路用戶比31到49歲的族群更經常使用無線設備。
Conclusion	Therefore, it can be assumed that young people are leading the use of wireless Internet.	因此，我們可以假定年輕族群是無線設備的最大用戶。

In presentation

③　It has been observed that Internet users under the age of 30 are more likely to use wireless devices than people between the ages of 31 and 49; so it's safe to assume that young people are driving the use of wireless Internet.

根據觀察，30歲以下的網路用戶比31到49歲的族群更經常使用無線設備，所以我們可以假定年輕族群是無線設備的最大用戶。

D

Premise	After receiving the drug for 17 days, the disabled mice could recognize objects and navigate mazes as well as the healthy mice.	在服用17天的藥後，智能缺損的老鼠開始能像健康的老鼠一樣辨別物體，並穿梭於迷宮之間。
Conclusion	The drug appeared to improve memory and learning in disabled mice and possibly in other small mammals.	因此，若該種藥品能增進智能缺損老鼠的記憶與學習能力，也許在其他小型哺乳類動物身上也會有相同效果。

In presentation

④　After receiving the drug for 17 days, the disabled mice could recognize objects and navigate mazes as well as the healthy mice. The results of the study suggest that this drug can improve memory and learning in other small mammals.

一項研究顯示在服用17天的藥後，智能缺損的老鼠開始能像健康老鼠一樣辨別物體，並穿梭於迷宮之間。這項研究顯示，該藥品或許也能增進其它小型哺乳類動物的記憶與學習能力。

6 Building up to a point you support/oppose
將論點歸結至贊成或反對的立場

你可以列舉一連串的論點，最終再把它們**歸納成一個你贊成或反對的結論**。這個舉動可以加強結論的真實性，也能讓聽眾印象深刻。

此方法在於先提出一些和論點相關的資訊，然後在結尾的最後一句加上一段贊成或反對的總結，其內容以簡潔有力為主，就算只有一個重點也無所謂。

結論 Step 1 ▶ 使用先前幾個 Unit 學到的技巧

① Taipei offers a great mix of the old and new: Interesting traditional curiosities and plenty of modern marvels are equally abundant, often in very close proximity. Also, public transportation is excellent, and escaping the urban jungle is never difficult because there are many large, beautiful parks and rural areas in and around the city.

台北是新與舊的融合：傳統的有趣珍寶和隨處可見的現代奇蹟往往同在一處。除此之外，大眾交通十分便利，市區美觀的大型公園和鄰近的郊區風光，讓市民可輕易享受都市叢林之外的景致。

結論 Step 2 ▶ 使用簡短、強調語氣的結語

② **In short**, I love this city!　　　　　　　總之，我超愛這座城市的！

更多例句

③ **Basically**, the performance was terrible!　　基本上，這場表演糟透了！

④ **Simply put**, it's amazing!　　　　　　　簡單來說，這實在太神奇了！

⑤ **To put it briefly**, everybody is happy!　　簡單地說，大家都很開心！

⑥ **To sum up**, sales were phenomenal!　　　總結算來，銷售量很驚人！

⑦ **In a nutshell**, it's a disaster!　　　　　概括來說，這是一場災難！

⑧ **In a word**, excellent!　　　　　　　　一言以蔽之，非常好！

⑨ **All in all**, it was totally revolutionary!　　總而言之，這是一大創新！

結論 Step **3** ▶ 反諷技巧

　　另一種歸納論點的方式是使用**反諷技巧**（ironic twist），它能幫助你的論點刺激聽眾的想法，並挑戰他們的觀點。這種方法需要先列出相關要點，鋪陳看似合理的理論，但卻在結尾最後以簡短又具強調性質的論據加以反駁。

● 先提出相關要點

⑩ The product features an innovative design, and the customer feedback we've received has been very positive. Plus, our advertising reaches more consumers than ever before.

這項產品擁有創新的設計，從顧客身上接收到的皆是正面的回饋。此外，產品廣告也比以往推廣給更多消費者認識。

● 再加以反駁

⑪ **And yet** the product still isn't selling!　但這項產品仍未上市。

更多例句

⑫ **The problem is** financing.　　這個問題出在財政。

⑬ **In spite of** these benefits, the program still failed.　　儘管有這些優點，這個計劃仍舊失敗了。

⑭ **But what I want to know is**, how does the new design benefit the user?　　但我想要知道的是，這項全新的設計如何造福使用者？

⑮ **So why is it that** nobody wants to join us?　　所以為何沒有人想要加入我們？

⑯ **So how come** we've failed the competition?　　所以為什麼我們會在這場競爭中失敗？

⑰ **Despite** these efforts, the plan backfired.　　儘管做了努力，這項計畫還是失敗了。

⑱ **Regardless of past failures**, this time was a total success.　　雖然過去失敗了，這次我們獲得了全然的成功。

① **The situation is bad!** Think about what has happened over the last two months. First, we had to downsize and lost the Taichung and Hsinchu branches. Next, there was the fire in the Tainan plant. The most recent blow has been the rise in our insurance premiums.

我們的狀況糟透了。想想前兩個月內所遭遇的事。第一,我們得縮編並撤掉台中和新竹分公司;接著,台南工廠發生火災;而最近的慘事是我們的保費被提高了。

② **Simply put, we succeeded!** I definitely think we sold the audience with our presentation. For starters, there was a lot of enthusiasm about the product and its potential. In the question-and-answer period, the audience had nothing but good things to say about the new design, the packaging, and the colors.

簡單來說,我們成功了!我認為聽眾們十分喜歡我們的簡報。首先,場內洋溢著一股對新產品和其潛力的期待氣氛;在提問的階段,聽眾們更對新設計、包裝和色彩讚不絕口。

③ **In short, we can't be beat!** We're giving you a lot of things that the other company can't offer. First, there's the money-back guarantee. Try it out; there's no risk whatsoever. Second, we have the only brand that features the total technology package.

簡單來說，我們是不會屈服的！我們提供你們許多其他公司無法提供的服務，第一，我們有退款保證，試試看，反正你們也沒有損失；第二，我們是唯一一家以提供完整資訊系統為特色的公司。

④ **Despite the bad press, we're leading the industry, and the market is strong!** The critics didn't like the product at all. They said we would be out of business by the end of the year and that the market would be saturated with cheap imitations.

儘管傳出負面新聞，我們仍穩坐此產業的龍頭，市場也依然蓬勃！評論家一點也不喜歡我們的產品，他們說我們年底前就會倒閉，而市面上會充斥著仿冒品。

⑤ **What we don't have is money.** We have the technology, we have the vision, and we have the personnel.

我們缺乏的是資金，我們有技術、有目標、也有人力。

UNIT 22 Linking the Parts of Your Presentation
連結簡報的各個部分

如果你能清楚連結簡報的各個部分，聽眾就能不費吹灰之力地了解你的論點。
每當你要進行到下一個新的主題時，可以直接向聽眾告知。

★ **結束**目前的主題

① That **completes/concludes** the media analysis.

媒體分析的部分已經**結束了**。

② **So that's all I have to say about** the research methods.

所以以上就是**關於**研究方法的部分。

③ **OK. So that does it for** the special features.

好，那是**關於**特別功能的部分。

★ **開始**一段新的主題

④ **So now we come to** the design part.

我們現在說到設計的部分。

⑤ **Now I'd like to describe** the experiment.

現在我要**敘述**的是實驗本身。

⑥ **OK. Now let's move on to** the market survey.

好，**現在要開始**介紹市場調查。

★ 收尾目前的主題，同時為下個主題開頭

⑦ **So that's it for** the problems; **now I'd like to** offer some solutions.

所以問題的部分**結束了**，**現在我想**提供給一些解決的方案。

⑧ **That's it for** the disadvantages. **I'll move on now** to the advantages.

缺點的部分**結束了**，**現在**我們來談談優點。

⑨ **Well, that ends** the background information; **so now I'll turn to** the technical specifications.

背景資訊的部分在此**做結了**，**我現在要來說明**詳細技術規格。

⑩ **So we've gone over** all the options; **let's turn now to** the pros and cons of each one.

所以我們已經敘述過所有選項，**現在我們將**討論各項的優點與缺點。

⑪ **So those are** the three choices. **Now I'll talk about** the pros and cons of each one.

所以我們有三種選擇，**現在我要分析**每種選擇的優缺點。

⑫ **OK. So that does it for** the evidence. **Next, I'll outline** the main points.

好的，例證的部分**講完了**。**接下來**，**我要列出**主要論點。

⑬ **Well, that concludes** the data on the present scenario; **so now I'll turn to** the outlook for the long term.

嗯……以上結束了目前現狀的數據，**現在我要談論的是**長遠的展望。

⑭ **So that's the end of** the first part. **Now I'll move on to** part two.

第一部分**結束了**，**現在我要講**第二部分。

Signposting
標明主題

清楚標明主題能引導聽眾順利進入簡報的其他部分。接下來將介紹這類用語，
讓你能輕鬆開始其他部分的報告。

1. Limiting the scope 限制討論範圍
2. Referring back 回顧之前提到的要點
3. Referring forward 列出之後才會提出的論點

Limiting the scope 限制討論範圍

有時候或許會因為時間、資料缺乏、訊息對聽眾過於艱深或其他理由，
想要限制簡報討論的範圍。

① **The** emulsification **process** is quite complicated, **so I won't discuss**
the technical details **today**.

乳化作用**的過程**十分複雜，**所以我今天不會**就技術細節**多討論**。

② **Given the time available** to me today, **I won't be able to go into**
greater detail on the legal ramifications.

就今天**現有的時間來說**，**我不會針對**法律各領域的細項討論。

③ **Without going into** technical detail, **it is possible to** explain the
broad principles of the theory of relativity.

即使沒有講解技術層面，**還是能夠**利用廣義的原理說明相對論。

④ String **theory is** quite complicated, **so I won't discuss** the technical
details today.

弦**理論**十分複雜，因此**我**今日**不會**對其原理細節**進行討論**。

⑤ **Given** the personal nature of these details, **I won't be able to** go into
greater detail about the patient.

由於這些議題細節的內容屬私人範疇，**我不便**太詳細討論這位患者的狀況。

2 Referring back 回顧之前提到的要點

回顧之前曾討論的論點，有時也能提供給聽眾一些相關資訊。

⑥ **As I said before**, all the taxes have been paid.
如同之前所說的，所有稅金都已經付清了。

⑦ **As I said in the introduction**, this law doesn't apply to our case.
如同我在介紹時說的，這條法規不適用於這個案子。

⑧ **As we've already seen**, the experiment proves the hypothesis.
如同我們之前看到的，這項實驗已經證實了假設。

⑨ **As I said in the previous part**, the new office is 45 ping.
如同我在上個部分提到的，新辦公室有45坪。

⑩ **As I mentioned earlier**, the market survey was inconclusive.
如同我之前提到的，此市場調查幫助不大。

3 Referring forward 列出之後才會提出的論點

簡報進行時，你也可能會先提出一個需要稍後進行解釋的論點。這項技巧和「限制討論範圍」很相似，因為它對目前應該討論的要點做出限制，但比較不同的是，聽眾知道他們在稍後的簡報中，就能得此論點的論述。

⑪ I'll explain this theory in more detail **in the next section**.
我將會**在下一個階段**進行更詳細的解說。

⑫ I'll **expand on** this idea **again later** when I talk about the case studies.
我將在稍後談論個案時，**再次詳述**這個概念。

⑬ This topic will **come up again later** in the marketing part of my presentation.
這個主題會在待會簡報進行至行銷部分時，**再被提出來討論**。

⑭ I'll **go into further detail** on water pollution toward the end of the presentation.
在簡報的尾聲，我會就水汙染這件事**做更細節的討論**。

UNIT 24 Making Predictions
對結果進行預測

要對未來的結果進行預測，需要使用**未來式**，以及形容「**可能性**」的修飾詞語。

1. Guaranteed to happen 一定會發生
2. Likely to happen 有可能發生
3. Uncertain 不確定
4. Unlikely to happen 不太可能發生
5. Definitely will not happen 絕對不會發生

1 Guaranteed to happen 一定會發生

① Orders will **definitely** increase soon. 訂單數量**一定**很快就會增加了。

② It's **certain** that orders will increase soon. 我**確信**訂單數量很快就會增加。

③ Orders will increase soon, that's **for sure**. 我**有把握**，訂單數量很快就會增加。

④ **There is no doubt** that orders will increase soon. **無疑地**，訂單數量很快就會增加。

⑤ The effects of the drought will **undoubtedly** continue until August. 乾旱的影響**無疑**會持續到八月。

2 Likely to happen 有可能發生

⑥ Orders will **probably** increase soon. 訂單數量**也許**很快就會增加了。

⑦ Orders will **likely** increase soon. 訂單數量**可能**很快就會增加了。

⑧ Orders **should** increase soon. 訂單數量**應該**很快會增加。

⑨ **In all likelihood**, orders will be increasing soon. 訂單數量將**很有可能**會很快上升。

3 Uncertain 不確定

⑩ Orders **may or may not** increase soon. **It's difficult to predict now.**

訂單**可能**很快就會增加，**也可能不會**。現在很難做出預測。

⑪ Orders **could** increase soon, **but they might not. It's hard to say at this point.**

訂單**可能**很快會增加，但也可能不會，現在說還太早。

4 Unlikely to happen 不太可能發生

⑫ Orders **probably won't** increase **anytime soon.**

訂單數量**可能短時間不會**增加。

⑬ If orders were to increase soon, **it would be a miracle.**

如果訂單數量能很快就增加，**將會是個奇蹟**。

⑭ The chance that orders will increase soon **is pretty slim.**

訂單數量要在短時間增加的**機會非常低**。

⑮ **Odds are** that orders **won't** increase soon.

訂單數量馬上增加的**機率不高**。

5 Definitely will not happen 絕對不會發生

⑯ **There's no chance** that orders will increase soon.

訂單要馬上增加的**機率為零**。

⑰ Orders **definitely won't** increase soon.

訂單在短時間**絕對不會**增加。

⑱ Orders **won't** increase. **It's impossible.**

訂單**不會**增加了。這是**不可能**的。

⑲ **Hell will freeze over before** orders increase.

訂單增加是**永遠不可能**的事。

⑳ **There's no way** their invention will win the award.

他們的發明**不可能**會得獎的。

UNIT 25 Making Recommendations
向聽眾提供建議

重點都說完後,可以對聽眾做不同程度的建議,讓他們在聽完演說後能親自實踐簡報的內容。

★ 向聽眾**提供建議**時,可以使用「**suggest**」或「**recommend**」等字彙。

① I **suggest** you buy the stock immediately.

我**建議**你馬上買下這支股票。

② Having compared all the pros and cons, my **suggestion** is to close the plant.

在比較所有的優缺點後,我的**建議**是關閉工廠。

③ After carefully analyzing all the data, I **recommend** adopting the new strategy.

在仔細分析所有資料後,我**推薦**採用新的策略。

④ My **recommendation** is that you open a branch in Dubai.

我的**建議**是,去杜拜開設新的分公司。

★ 使用「**should**」能幫助你省略不必要的敘述,向聽眾**直接論述重點**。

⑤ You **should** sell everything now while the price is still high.

你**應該**趁現在價格很高的時候把它們全部賣掉。

⑥ The company **should** fire the consultant as soon as possible.

公司**應該**盡快將那名顧問開除。

⑦ You **should** penetrate deeper into the small to medium business segment.

你**應該**更深入了解中小型企業體系。

★ 你個人的**專業意見**也足夠成為他人的建議。

⑧ **In my opinion,** the answer is obvious: Hire the candidate with the most relevant experience.

就我看來，答案再簡單也不過了：雇用一位最具有相關經驗的應徵者。

⑨ **From my point of view**, the deal seems equally advantageous for both sides.

以我的觀點看來，這筆交易似乎對雙方都是有利的。

⑩ The best way to reduce oil imports and carbon emissions over the next decade, **in my opinion**, is through increased use of biofuels.

減少未來幾十年石油進口和碳排放量的最佳方式，**依我看來**，是透過增加生物燃料的使用。

★ 若建議是很**急迫**的，你可以使用更強烈的用字像「**must**」或「**have to**」。

⑪ To survive in this rapidly changing industry, companies **must** adjust their strategies.

為了要在快速變遷的企業生存下去，每家公司**必須**改變它們的策略。

⑫ The world's top polluter **must** become the pioneer in reducing carbon dioxide output from coal-burning power plants.

全球最高汙染的企業**必須**成為先鋒，減少因火力發電而排放的二氧化碳。

⑬ To overcome this technical problem, we **have to** commit more resources to R&D.

要解決這個技術問題，我們**必須**花更多心力在研發上。

⑭ There aren't many job opportunities in Texas, so you **have to** move somewhere else.

德州已沒有太多的工作機會，因此你**得**搬家到外地。

PART 5

PHRASES FOR CONCLUDING YOUR PRESENTATION

總結簡報的語句

強而有力的簡報結論，需要一段清楚重申主旨的概述（summary）；
若有必要，也可以用疑問句做結。

UNIT 26 Concluding With a Summary
用概述做結論

當簡報要結束時，你必須以主旨明確的概述收尾，讓聽眾重新複習簡報的重點。

使用以下的總結語例句，說明自己的主要論點（main points）；也可搭配〈Unit 20〉中的例句一起使用。

① So **to sum up**, the most important thing is to cut costs. **First, we must** . . .

總結來說，首要之務就是降低成本。**首先，我們一定要**……

② **To summarize**, we need to work on providing better service for the customer. **To begin with**, . . .

總結來說，我們必須努力提供給顧客更好的服務。**首先**……

③ **Before closing, I'd like to briefly go through my main points again.** This product is especially useful for business travelers. **For starters**, . . .

在結尾前，我會再次簡單重述我的主要論點。這個產品特別適合商業旅客使用，**首先**……

EXAMPLES 67

A

> **Main idea**

Acme's server platform offers advanced technology.

尖端公司的伺服器平台提供高階科技服務。

> **Sub-point ❶**

How will each component improve your company's efficiency?

平台的各個環節會如何改善貴公司的工作效率。

> **Sub-point ❷**

Acme's server technology is more advanced than its competitors' on all the key comparison points.

尖端伺服器科技公司在各個層面都比其他競爭者卓越。

> **Sub-point ❸**

Acme beats other companies on price.

尖端伺服器科技公司在價位上也比其他公司好。

> **Summary**

① **To summarize**, Acme offers the most advanced technology on the market today. **Firstly**, each and every component of this fabulous platform will vastly improve your company's IT efficiency, consolidate your management, and reduce the need for on-site service calls. **Secondly**, keep in mind that Acme's server technology handily beats its competitors' products on every key comparison point. **Lastly**, Acme's ultra-low price is unheard of.

總結來說，尖端伺服器科技公司提供此產業中最先進的技術。**第一**、此優秀平台的每一項環節都將大幅度地增進貴公司資訊部的效率，加強管理，並減少客服電話。**第二**、尖端伺服器科技公司於各個重要層面都遙遙領先其他競爭者。**最後**，尖端伺服器科技公司的超低價位也絕對是前所未有的。

Ⓑ

Main idea

Our agency offers improved marketing strategies.

敝公司提供提升行銷策略的服務。

Sub-point ①

Our agency stays on top of the latest trends in marketing.

敝公司深諳行銷策略，是業界的潮流先鋒。

Sub-point ②

Our agency uses focus groups to determine important goals for each company.

敝公司利用焦點團體來訂定各公司的重要目標。

Sub-point ③

Our agency has satisfied many clients by developing successful marketing campaigns.

敝公司有許多滿意的客戶，並有許多成功的商業行銷經驗。

Summary

② **So now, I'd like to go through my main points. To begin with,** our agency stays on top of the latest trends in marketing, ensuring that the client's message is always current. **Next**, we use focus groups to determine the most important goals for each company. **Finally**, we have satisfied many clients with our highly successful marketing campaigns.

現在，讓我再重述之前的論點。**首先**，敝公司深諳行銷策略，在業界首屈一指，確保您的行銷內容領先潮流。**接著**，敝公司利用焦點團體來訂定客戶的重要目標。**最後**，敝公司有許多滿意的客戶，並有許多成功的商業行銷經驗。

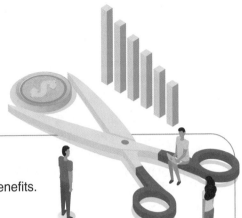

Main idea

Downsizing offers many benefits.

公司縮編有許多好處。

Sub-point 1

Overhead can be reduced.

可以降低成本。

Sub-point 2

Funds can be reinvested more productively.

資金可以更有效地再被投資。

Sub-point 3

The benefits are both real and long term.

這些好處不但實質且長遠。

Summary

③ **I'll conclude now with a summary of my main ideas. The first point is that** with our innovative ideas, downsizing can significantly reduce your overhead and save you a lot of money. **The second point** is that capital can be reinvested more productively. **Lastly**, there are fantastic long-term benefits.

我要來總結方才提到的重點。**第一**，我們對於公司縮編有許多創新的想法，可以降低成本並縮減大筆預算。**第二**，資金可以更有效地再被投資。**最後**，將會有絕佳的長期益處。

UNIT 27
Inviting Questions and Responding to Them
邀請提問並加以回應

問答階段可以使聽眾有機會表達自己不清楚的地方，也使演說者有機會了解自己的不足或重申立場。

1. Inviting questions 邀請提問
2. Being unable to answer 無法回應
3. Asking for clarification before answering 回應問題前先請發問者澄清問題
4. Agreeing/Disagreeing 贊同／不贊同
5. Providing reassurance 給予保證

1 Inviting questions 邀請提問

1. Any questions?

   有任何問題嗎？

2. So, are there any questions?

   那各位有什麼問題嗎？

3. I'd like to thank you for listening, and if there are any questions, I'd be happy to answer them now.

   感謝各位的聆聽，如果有任何問題，我很樂意現在就來為各位回答。

2 Being unable to answer 無法回應

若你無法回應聽眾的提問，你可以用以下的語句回答。

1. I'm afraid I don't have that information. If you leave your email address with me, I'll get back to you on that.

   很抱歉，我沒有其相關資料。請留下您的 email，我稍後會和您聯繫。

2. I can't answer that question at the moment, but I can get the answer for you later. Can you leave your phone number with me?

   我現在無法立刻回答這個問題，但稍後會答覆您。能否請您留下電話？

③ I'm not an expert on that subject, but I can forward your question to one of my colleagues.

我不是這方面的專家，但我能將問題轉達給我的同事。

3 Asking for clarification before answering
回應問題前先請發問者澄清問題

　　當你對問題有疑問時，可以要求提問者再次加以澄清。你也可能是因為沒聽清楚提問者的問題而產生疑慮。

① Sorry, could you repeat the question? I couldn't quite hear you.

很抱歉，能請您重複一次問題嗎？我沒有聽清楚。

② Sorry, I didn't hear you. Could you say that again, please?

很抱歉，我沒有聽見您的問題，可以請您重述一次嗎？

　　如果你認為已經聽清楚問題，只是沒有很確定，你可以向提問者**重述問題，再做一次確認**。

③ Are you asking me to explain how the process applies to the commercial market segment?

您的問題是要我解釋它是如何應用於商業市場的步驟嗎？

④ Did I hear you correctly? Did you ask why we haven't sold the publishing rights?

我有聽錯嗎？您剛剛是問我們公司為何尚未出售版權？

　　提問的問題或許太籠統，很難給予一個具有意義的答覆。在這種情況下，你可以**請提問者將問題具體化**。

⑤ When you say "the Pacific Ocean," which part are you referring to?

您剛提到「太平洋」，是指它的哪個部分？

⑥ You said, "the future." Do you mean the near future or the long term?

您説到「未來」，是指未來幾年還是長遠來看？

⑦ By "next year," do you mean early or late in the year?

所謂「明年」，是指上半年或是下半年？

217

提出的問題會牽涉到你**贊成或反對該論點**。

① Agreed.
我同意。

② I couldn't agree more.
我相當贊同。

③ I absolutely agree with you.
我完全贊同您的看法。

....

你或許還會加上你**同意的原因**為何。

④ I have the same opinion. Let me explain why.
我持相同立場。讓我解釋原因。

⑤ I completely concur. In fact, there is evidence showing . . .
我完全同意這點。實際上有足夠的論證證明……

⑥ I'm with you on this one. The study clearly indicates . . .
我同意您的說法。這項研究充分顯示……

....

你或許也會和提問者持相反意見。一方面，你可以**用圓滑的語句表達對問題的尊重**。

⑦ I see your point, but have you considered the other side of the argument?
我了解您的立場，但您是否有考慮過另一種論點？

⑧ I have some doubts about what you're saying. I don't think you have all the facts.
我對您的論述有一些疑慮，我認為您可能沒有掌握全部的實際狀況。

⑨ What you're saying is partly true; but really, I have to disagree.
您剛所說的部分屬實，但我仍不同意您的看法。

另一方面，你也許會遇到太激動和沒禮貌的提問者。如果是這樣，你可以試著要**提問者冷靜下來**。

⑩ Please calm down. I'm sorry you feel that way, but I still disagree.

請您冷靜一點。我很抱歉讓您有這種感受，但我還是不認同您的看法。

⑪ I think we're at an impasse. Can we just agree to disagree on this point?

我想我們陷入僵局了。也許我們能同意彼此對這件事持有相反立場？

⑫ I'm afraid getting angry won't help. I still can't agree with your point of view.

我很抱歉，但生氣並不能解決這件事，而我還是必須和您持相反意見。

5 Providing reassurance 給予保證

提問者也許對某些論點有疑慮，並希望你能提出讓他們消除疑慮的保證。

① I understand your concern. But let me assure you, there is nothing to worry about.

我了解您的疑慮，但我向您保證，沒有什麼好擔心的。

② Seriously, you don't have to worry about that at all.

說真的，您完全不必擔心那些。

③ That's a valid concern, but I guarantee that we'll take care of it for you.

這是合理的懷疑，但我向您保證，我們會替您完善處理。

①

Are there any questions you'd like me to answer now?

你們有任何問題並希望我在現在回答的嗎？

Yeah, I have a question. I'd like to know what you're going to do about the number of feral cats at the beach.

是的，我有一個疑問。我想知道您對於海灘上的流浪貓有什麼因應方式？

We don't have a specific plan for dealing with the cats right now, but I know it's on the list of issues to be addressed this year.

對於流浪貓這件事我們還沒研擬出因應方式，但我知道這是今年待解決的事情之一。

Are you aware that spaying and neutering is more effective than extermination at controlling feral cat populations?

您是否同意結紮流浪貓比撲殺牠們更能有效控制流浪貓的數量？

I totally agree with that idea. Let me assure you that I'll pass it on to the group working on this important problem.

我完全同意這想法，我會將這意見轉告負責處理這個重要問題的小組。

So, are there any questions?
所以，有任何問題嗎？

Yes, I have a question. Will the damage to the manufacturing plant from the earthquake affect next year's production?
是的，我有一個問題。明年的生產量會因地震造成的廠房毀損而有所影響嗎？

When you say "next year," could you be more specific?
請問您說的「明年」是確切指何時？

Can you give us a quarterly production estimate?
您可以指出每一季的預估生產量嗎？

Sorry. I don't have that information right now, but if you leave your email address, I'll send the data to you.
抱歉，我現在手上沒有相關資訊。但如果您留email給我，我會將該數據寄給您。

UNIT 28 Saying Thank You and Goodbye
致謝並道別

當所有問題已經提問完畢，簡報也該畫下句點。現在你的最後任務就是答謝聽眾，並且好好道別。

① No more questions? OK. Then **thank you** all very much for your attention this morning, and I **look forward to** seeing you again next year.

沒有問題了嗎？好，非常**感謝**各位早上的聆聽，我**期待**明年再與各位會面。

② Any other problems? No? OK then. **Thanks** for your interest in our product. My contact information is on the handout in case you have any concerns later. **Goodbye.**

還有其他問題嗎？沒有的話，非常**感謝**各位對我們產品的關切，如果有任何問題，可以從剛才發放的資料上找到我的聯絡資訊。**再見。**

③ Are there any more questions? None at all? All right then. **I'd like to thank you all once again for coming!**

各位還有問題嗎？都沒有嗎？很好。**我想要再次感謝各位的蒞臨！**

④ Anybody else have any concerns? No? Fine then. I'd just like to say **thanks for** your participation and **I look forward to seeing you all again next year**. Please enjoy the rest of your time here in Taiwan.

還有人有其他疑慮嗎？沒有？好的。我想**大大地感謝你們**，也**很期待明年能再見到各位**，祝你們接下來在台灣的時間玩得愉快。

⑤ So are there any further questions? None? Really? **I'll finish here then**. **Thank you** all for coming, and have a pleasant journey home.

還有其他的問題嗎？一個都沒有嗎？真的嗎？**那麼今天的演講就到此結束了**，**感謝**各位的蒞臨並祝大家回程旅途愉快。

商務英文簡報 技巧全攻略
Making Presentations in English

作 者	Ian Andrew McKinnon	
審 訂	Judy Majewski	
翻 譯	羅竹君／鄭家文	
校 對	歐寶妮	
編 輯	楊維芯／王鈺婷	
主 編	丁宥暄	
內 文 排 版	陳瀅竹／蔡怡柔	
版 型 設 計	陳瀅竹	
封 面 設 計	林書玉	
製 程 管 理	洪巧玲	
出 版 者	寂天文化事業股份有限公司	
發 行 人	黃朝萍	
電 話	+886-(0)2-2365-9739	
傳 真	+886-(0)2-2365-9835	
網 址	www.icosmos.com.tw	
讀 者 服 務	onlineservice@icosmos.com.tw	
出 版 日 期	2022 年11月 初版二刷 （寂天雲隨身聽APP版）	

國家圖書館出版品預行編目(CIP)資料

商務英文簡報技巧全攻略 (寂天雲隨身聽 APP) /
Ian Andrew McKinnon 著 ; 羅竹君 , 鄭家文翻譯 . --
初版 . -- [臺北市] : 寂天文化事業股份有限公司 ,
2022.11 印刷
　　面 ；　公分
　ISBN 978-626-300-166-4 (25K 平裝)

　1.CST: 商業英文 2.CST: 讀本 3.CST: 簡報

　805.18　　　　　　　　　111017450